Had he seen

Deanna quickene

'So, Miss Sullivan.' Taut menace shadowed the sharply honed lines of Alejo de Rocas's face. 'We meet again.'

He must have moved like lightning! He caught Deanna's hunted look with grim satisfaction. 'Had you thought to avoid me a second time?' he gritted, his voice gravelly, deep, rippling along her nervous system. 'A wasted hope, my beautiful, treacherous deceiver. I warned you that I would return...'

THIS BOOK MAY BE PART EXCHANGED
IF IN GOOD CONDITION AT:
BOBBIES BOOKSHOP
220 MORRISON STREET
EDINBURGH EH3 8EA
50 p.

Dear Reader

There's nothing more wonderful than celebrating the end of winter, with an exciting collection of books to choose from! Mills & Boon will transport you to all corners of the world, including two enchanting Euromance destinations—sun-drenched, exotic Madeira contrasting with scenic evergreen Wales. Let the spring sunshine brighten up your day by reading our romances which are bursting with love and laughter! So why not treat yourself to many hours of happy reading?

The Editor

When **Joanna Neil** discovered Mills & Boon, her lifelong addiction to reading crystallised into an exciting new career—writing romances. Always prey to a self-indulgent imagination, she loved to give free rein to her characters, who were probably the outcome of her varied lifestyle. She has been a clerk, telephonist, typist, nurse and infant teacher. She enjoys dressmaking and cooking at her Leicestershire home. Her family includes a husband, son and daughter, an exuberant yellow Labrador, and two slightly crazed cockatiels.

Recent titles by the same author:

FLAME OF LOVE

DEVIL'S QUEST

BY
JOANNA NEIL

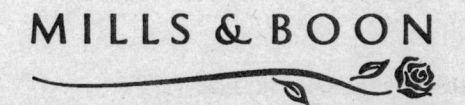

MILLS & BOON

MILLS & BOON LIMITED
ETON HOUSE, 18-24 PARADISE ROAD
RICHMOND, SURREY TW9 1SR

All the characters in this book have no existence outside the imagination of the Author, and have no relation whatsoever to anyone bearing the same name or names. They are not even distantly inspired by any individual known or unknown to the Author, and all the incidents are pure invention.

All Rights Reserved. The text of this publication or any part thereof may not be reproduced or transmitted in any form or by any means, electronic or mechanical, including photocopying, recording, storage in an information retrieval system, or otherwise, without the written permission of the publisher.

This book is sold subject to the condition that it shall not, by way of trade or otherwise, be lent, resold, hired out or otherwise circulated without the prior consent of the publisher in any form of binding or cover other than that in which it is published and without a similar condition including this condition being imposed on the subsequent purchaser.

*First published in Great Britain 1994
by Mills & Boon Limited*

© Joanna Neil 1994

*Australian copyright 1994
Philippine copyright 1994
This edition 1994*

ISBN 0 263 78425 8

*Set in Times Roman 11 on 12 pt.
01-9403-49166 C*

Made and printed in Great Britain

CHAPTER ONE

'WHAT'S wrong, Luis? Please tell me.' Deanna Sullivan frowned unhappily as her dark-haired companion cast yet another wary, searching glance around the crowded square. 'I know you're in some kind of trouble and I want to know what's going on.'

'I can't talk about it—not yet,' Luis said. 'It would not be fair to burden you with my problems.'

'But you're planning on leaving,' Deanna protested. 'How can you do that? What about your job? You're in the middle of cataloguing a collection, aren't you?'

He grimaced. 'It is not working out as I expected. There are people in this business who cannot be trusted, and I—— *Dios*!' His eyes narrowed in laser-like concentration. 'What is he doing here?'

'Who?' Deanna jumped at his sharp exclamation. 'Is it one of the men who are following you?' She watched anxiously, as he made a strategic retreat around the back of the laden flower cart, hiding himself behind the blooms that decorated its roof supports.

'I have not seen them. I think they have not yet caught up with me.' He drew in a deep breath, his knuckles pressed hard and white against the wood of the painted wagon.

'*Perdoneme.*' Deanna knelt to retrieve the fronds of greenery that had drifted to the floor, apologising to the young Peruvian flower seller who looked on in alarm at the desecration of her carefully arranged display. 'Luis, whatever is the matter? Tell me. If you're in danger, I'll go and fetch the police.'

'No.' His voice was taut. 'I do not want them involved. Not yet. Be still, Deanna. I need a moment to think.'

Deanna subsided, her gaze restively sweeping the crowded plaza for some sign of the man who had caused her companion's sudden unease. His mood was at such odds with the pleasurable, festive atmosphere about them; it was out of place on a day when it seemed that everyone had turned out to enjoy the fiesta in the warm sunshine.

The brightly costumed procession was winding its way around the square, dancers moving to the throbbing beat of guitars, encouraged by the lively, energetic rhythm of the chicha music. There was laughter and singing, and the air was heavy with the scent of thousands of blossoms, their bold colours of scarlet, azure and gold vying for attention. Palm trees, set at neat intervals among the flat paving stones, desultorily waved their green foliage in the faint breeze.

Turning back to Luis, Deanna sent a swift, searching glance over his tense frame.

'I wish you would tell me what's going on,' she pressed urgently. 'I want to help.'

'It is best you do not know,' he said. 'That way you can come to no harm.'

Deanna's jaw made an obstinate slant. 'Stop fudging, Luis,' she commanded. 'How long have we known each other? Years, off and on. We go way back, and if you're in some kind of trouble I want to do whatever I can to help you sort it out.' Once more she scanned the seething crowd. 'Who is this man? Is he dangerous?'

'He is Alejo de Rocas.' His mouth twisted in a tight grimace. 'At this moment, he could well be bad news for me.'

She frowned, looking at him in some confusion. 'But he's your employer, isn't he? I thought he was in the States—didn't you tell me he was away for a few weeks?—and why should you be trying to avoid him? What have you done?'

'I have done nothing wrong, you must believe me, Deanna. But I cannot expect that Señor de Rocas will take my word on that. I have worked for him for just a few months, and his mind has been poisoned against me, I think. I must have time to prove myself, to show that I am innocent. He must not find me here.'

'But you can't seriously mean to go tearing off across country without giving the matter a lot more thought,' Deanna said, trying to be coolly practical. 'If there's a problem, let the police deal with it.'

'You think they will take my word against that of Rocas, with all the evidence pointing against me? I am not such a fool.' His lips set in a firm line, and Deanna winced inwardly. That look was all too familiar; it was one that she had come to recognise over the years, and she knew that there was no reasoning with Luis in this frame of mind.

She had to try, though. 'What evidence? For heaven's sake, Luis, tell me what is going on. All I know is that you're in some desperate kind of trouble, and you're taking off on some wild journey as though the hounds of hell are hurtling after you. Why won't you explain?'

'I have no time. My taxi will be here at any minute now.'

Deanna shook her head, her shimmering honey-gold curls settling around her shoulders in a flurry of disorder. 'You could at least stay and try to iron things out with Señor de Rocas. He's bound to listen to you, to allow you a fair hearing.'

Luis laughed without humour. 'You do not know Alejo de Rocas. He did not earn the name "*Diablo*" without good cause. He can be ruthless, without mercy, as the devil himself. Those who have crossed him will testify to that.'

Deanna's finely shaped brows drew together. Luis must be exaggerating. It was the Latin temperament at work—he was under pressure. She repressed a sigh. Getting information out of him was like trying to prise open a clam.

'Where is he? Where did you see him?'

Luis gestured surreptitiously with his hand. 'Over there, the side-street near the entrance to the square. He was standing by his Range Rover—is he still there?'

Traffic was at a standstill on this day of festivity, the only access for vehicles being one or two streets that skirted the plaza, and Deanna peered along them. Her glance came joltingly to halt on the stark figure of a man, outlined against the backdrop of buff-coloured stone buildings.

There could be no mistaking him. His height alone was enough to catch the eye, but there was also an intimidating width of shoulder that gave her pause for thought. Beneath the faithful moulding of black shirt and black trousers, his tautly muscled frame gave the impression of steely strength.

She nodded slowly. 'Oh, yes,' she said, her voice a breath of sound. 'I see him.' Midnight hair crisply framed a tough-boned face, made harsh by the grim purpose etched into every angular line. His mouth was hard, its firmly rounded contours rigidly controlled.

In spite of the sun's caress on her bare arms, Deanna shivered. '*Diablo*,' she muttered, testing the sound of it on her tongue. The name was fitting.

The man's dark gaze raked over the assembled throng, searching with formidable intent, and she felt, with unholy certainty, that Luis was right, he would be a dangerous man to cross.

She turned away, pushing him determinedly from her thoughts, and said with soft insistence, 'Luis, you have to think again about rushing off this way. It's far too risky. You could get into all sorts of difficulties.'

'I have to go,' Luis said in fixed disregard. 'It would be even more hazardous to stay here, where I could be so easily found. There is too much danger. I dare not even take my own transport, for fear of recognition.'

'But surely——'

'No,' Luis cut in. 'My mind is made up. The taxi should be across the other side of the square in just a few minutes. All I have to think about is keeping out of Rocas's way. Is the coast clear? Has he gone?'

'Not yet.' Deanna looked unhappily towards the side-street. Alejo de Rocas was not a man who would be easily thwarted, she sensed it. He would pursue his goal with unyielding resolution, and she pitied anyone reckless enough to step in his way.

She slanted her gaze over his tall, powerfully masculine frame, sweeping upwards to contemplate the darkly rugged planes of his face, and then she froze. Her blue glance was captured and held fast, meshed with his in compelling union. A shock of prickling awareness rippled along the length of her spine. All sound faded into nothing; the clamour and frenzied activity in the square no longer had any existence as she absorbed the brooding intensity of his stare.

She could not break that contact. It was as though he had reached out across this crowded place and pinioned her with a force she did not comprehend.

Hazily, she became aware of some persistent intrusion slicing the bond that held her in thrall. At last Luis's strained tones penetrated the mists that fogged her brain. 'I must go,' he was saying. 'I'll have to slip through the crowd and hope that he does not see me. You could help—you could keep him from coming after me.'

With an effort, Deanna dragged her gaze away from that strongly magnetic hold, and turned her back on the tall, dark stranger. She tried to compose her thoughts into some sort of order. Luis wanted her to impede the devil, to hinder him in his black pursuit. Wasn't that what he had said—wasn't he asking the impossible? She pulled herself together.

'Whatever has happened, you must be able to talk it through in a civilised fashion. These are not the Dark Ages, after all. Are you absolutely certain you can't stay just long enough to hear what he has to say?'

'That would be a deadly move,' Luis retorted with deep conviction. 'He believes I have wronged him, and he will move heaven and earth to have me thrown into gaol. I have committed no crime, but Rocas will not listen; he will hunt me down without mercy. Until I can prove my innocence, I must stay away.'

Deanna frowned, her blue eyes troubled. 'Tell me what you're supposed to have done. Luis, I want——'

'I have already said too much. I must go. I have to meet the taxi at the rank by the concert hall. It will be coming from the north, through the hills.' He shot a hasty glance through the hanging flower blossoms. 'Good. He is not looking this way.' He began to edge out from behind the flower stall.

'But how shall I be able to contact you?' she queried anxiously. 'Where will you be?'

'Don't worry, I will phone you. For now, I'm going to travel east. Goodbye, Deanna.'

'But you——'

'It's all right. I know what I'm doing. If you want to help me, you could keep an eye on him for the next few minutes. If it looks as though he has seen me; do what you can to keep him from following me.'

Deanna watched helplessly as he made a slow, weaving path through the crowd, hindered several times by the merrymakers, jostled by Peruvians in huge, grinning masks. The taxi had not yet made its appearance on the far side of the square, and she hoped that Alejo de Rocas's attention would be diverted long enough for Luis to make his escape.

How could Luis have fallen into such dire straits? He was usually such an open, friendly man. She had known him for so long, and she could not imagine him doing anything in the slightest way dishonest. At one time, perhaps, infatuation might have coloured her judgement, she accepted that. When she had lived here some years back, when her father's job as a diplomat had brought them to this place, she and Luis had been constantly together, and she had thought the world of him. It would hardly have been unexpected for her to take his side. But that heady intoxication had been just a phase, she acknowledged; they had soon realised they were not suited to each other in that way. But their friendship had been cemented.

Even after her return to England, she recalled, the contact had not been broken. From time to time, he had written, kept her in touch with the way his life was going, let her know a little about his various romances. She had already known that he had graduated from Harvard, and later, when he had embarked on a further study tour, they had even shared some time together at her own university. Whenever he visited London, he made a point of seeking her out. He was like a brother to her, wasn't he? There was a strong bond between them, and she knew he could not have done anything wrong. She was sure of it. Instinct told her that there must be some mistake.

She sent a darting glance behind her, to the man who stood beside the Range Roger, and saw the sudden tensing of that lithe figure. Lord, he had seen Luis. She groaned aloud. What was she to do? His eyes followed Luis's movements beyond the square to where he waited for the taxi, homing in on him like a dark, intense bird of prey.

Rocas must have guessed what Luis had planned. How could she allow her friend to be pursued and beleaguered by such a man? Luis needed time alone to think things through.

She had to do something, quickly, but what? She looked around, searchingly. The cart—that might be the answer. If she could wheel it over——

Beside her, the flower seller tapped her feet in time to the music. 'Would you like to join in the dancing?' Deanna asked in fluent Spanish. 'I'll look after the cart if that's what you want. Here——' she thrust some money towards the young girl '—a deposit, for its safe return. Go and enjoy yourself.'

To her relief, the girl did not hesitate long. '*Gracias, señorita*, I would like that very much.'

Barely had she moved into the mêlée when Deanna lifted the painted wooden handles and began to trundle the heavy cart away from the stifling crowd towards the road where Señor de Rocas had been standing. He was tugging open the door of his vehicle. All he had to do was to take the first turning on his left, drive down the side-street and he would be able to negotiate the route to the taxi stand.

She looked around. In the far, far distance the jagged peaks of the Andes stretched long fingers across the skyline, a blue-grey backcloth for the green foothills that surrounded the small town. Winding a careful path around a tree-strewn hillside, the taxi that Luis waited for worked its way ever closer. Soon he would be starting safely on his journey. Alejo de Rocas would never make it in time if he pursued him on foot. The swaying, surging procession was even now twisting towards them, with its accompaniment of musicians and happy, cheering people. The side-street was his only answer, and if she could position the cart at the intersection, cut off his exit, there was no way he could reach Luis.

A few more yards, and she made it to the middle of the road. No one in their right mind was going to drive along here on this day of all days. It was a day for fun and relaxation, for letting go the pent-up tensions of everyday life. And no autocratic Peruvian with Spanish ancestry was going to make an exception, if she had anything to do with it.

Releasing the handles, she set the cart in place and straightened, breathing slowly to counter the nervous hammering of her heart. She ran her hands over the fullness of her cotton skirt, smoothing away imaginary creases in the soft folds of sprigged blue material. Turning around to face the square once more, she tried to ignore the slow approach of the Range Rover behind her.

The vehicle ground to a halt. A door slammed and the dark-haired stranger walked towards her, his tread brisk and purposeful. She braced herself.

'*Señorita*, you are blocking my way. You will move this contraption, *por favor*.'

He addressed her in concise, rapid Spanish, and she stared at him, blankly, pretending not to understand. Her slender fingers spread in a gesture of vague incomprehension, while her soft, full mouth tilted gently in a sweet smile of apology.

His head went back a fraction, a glimmer of something disturbing and unreadable flickering momentarily in the depths of his deep brown eyes.

'You want flowers?' she queried softly. 'For your sweetheart? Of course. Now, which sort would you prefer, I wonder?'

'Ah,' he muttered, enlightened. '*Inglesa.*'

She smiled again, and let her fingertips trail light as gossamer over the blooms. Thoughtfully, she held them poised for a few seconds, then plucked a heavy blossom from the fragrant mass, delicately twirling its long stem between her thumb and forefinger. With dreamy preoccupation, she trailed its pink-flushed petals over the soft golden skin of her cheek.

About to say something, he paused, a muscle jerking almost imperceptibly along the hard line of his jaw. 'No,' he said. 'I want——'

'Oh, I have it,' she murmured, 'you want something more exotic, more symbolic of passion and intensity. Let me see...'

This time, her fingers settled on a bloom that was vividly scarlet, but before she could remove it his bronzed hand swooped down and clamped her wrist. Her heartbeat kicked into chaotic action, a rapid pulse of sensation sweeping through her veins in a heated tide. Her flesh burned where he touched her. She drew in a swift breath, her gaze locking with his.

His eyes mocked her. Leaning closer, his chiselled, aristocratic features blocked out the light, so that she was only aware of height, and strength, and dangerous masculinity.

'I do not wish to buy flowers from you, *señorita*. I wish only that you would move this cart.' He spoke to her in perfect English.

Deanna looked down at the strong brown fingers that manacled her slender bones. 'You are hurting me,' she said, lifting blue eyes to challenge his own.

'*Lo siento.*' His voice was a deep rumble. He did not sound the least bit sorry.

Finding herself released, she began to carefully rearrange the blossoms. The taxi had not yet reached the pavement where Luis waited.

She said fixedly, 'I, too, am sorry. It's unfortunate that there is nothing here that appeals to your sensibilities, *señor*. These are, after all, the finest flowers in all of Cacheni. I think you'll find——'

'I did not say that there was nothing here to capture my attention.' His mouth made a faint curve, his gaze travelling over her in a glittering appraisal that brought a wave of hot colour to her cheeks. 'On the contrary. But I am in a hurry, *señorita*. Much as I might care to linger, there are matters of great urgency which demand my presence elsewhere.'

'I'm surprised to hear you say that,' Deanna persisted with determined obstinacy. 'The fiesta is a time for celebration, surely, a day for putting aside all the usual harassment of business dealings and such. Look at everyone out there...' She waved a hand towards the plaza. 'They're all out to have a good time. They've put their worries aside for a while. Perhaps you should do the same. Tomorrow is another day.'

'Tomorrow may be too late,' he said in a clipped tone. 'Please move the cart so that I can get by.'

'And shake up all these lovely blooms?' Deanna shook her head dismissively. 'Some of them have already lost petals, see? It was bad enough when people stumbled against them out there in the plaza. No, this place is much more peaceful, and out of the strong sun, too. The shade here is just right to keep them in perfect condition.'

He muttered something incomprehensible in Spanish, then seized the cart handles and pushed it on to the pavement. Deanna went after him.

'Now look what you've done,' she said crossly, standing in his path. 'Water splattered everywhere, leaves falling about all over the place—you have no idea what——'

Her diatribe came to a spluttering halt as his large hands settled firmly around her ribcage, and he lifted her bodily, swinging her up into the air. Open-mouthed, she clutched at his shoulders for support, staring down at the golden-tanned fingers which made such a bold contrast against the whiteness of her blouse.

'Put me down, this minute,' she demanded hotly. 'You have no right——'

He began to lower her, and all sensation was centred on the hot fusion of her soft curves against the hard wall of his chest as she slid to the ground. Shamingly, she felt her pulse thunder in startled, wilful reaction to the shocking contact. There was a roaring in her ears, a heady rush of blood as her senses careered out of control. Beneath her fingers she felt the strong muscles of his arms flexing, and then, confusingly, he was pushing her away from him, holding her at arm's length as he looked down into her dazed blue eyes.

'It is my deepest regret that I have to leave you, *señorita*,' he murmured, his gravelly voice sending strange quivers along her nervous system, 'but who knows? We may meet again. Tomorrow is, as you say, another day.' Then he let her go, and walked swiftly back to his vehicle.

Her mind was strangely blank. Her skin tingled still, her cheeks burning as though they were filled with hectic colour. Where his fingers had curved warmly around her ribcage, there was now only cold desolation. In just a few short moments, he had wreaked havoc with her senses, driven all conscious thought from her mind.

She blinked, trying to focus on her surroundings. A street, tall buildings on either side.

The sound of music and human energy in the background. Slowly, reality came back to her.

Luis. Had he escaped? She stared into the distance, watching the taxi move slowly away. Rounding a corner, the sun glinting off its gunmetal bodywork, was a sleek Range Rover. She released a long, pent-up breath. There was nothing more she could do. All she could hope for was that the taxi driver could somehow shake off the vehicle that followed in dogged pursuit.

Walking back to the hotel, she reflected that it might not have helped much even if she'd had her pick-up truck to hand. With it, she could have provided a temporary solution to Luis's problems, but she had a job to do at the Centre, and it simply wasn't feasible to go wandering about the country at a moment's notice. Not that he would have let her. He was determined on going alone, on keeping her out of it as far as possible.

The fact that the pick-up was out of action was a nuisance, but with a bit of luck it should be ready for collection from the garage tomorrow, once the festivities were over and done with. She could pick up the medical supplies for the Centre then, too. The fiesta had delayed everything, but it was no great problem to stay at the hotel overnight.

She wished she had some way of knowing what was happening, how Luis would fare. Perhaps, if all went well, he would contact her at work. She could be driving back there by lunchtime tomorrow, and if he called to say everything was back to normal these last few hours would become nothing more than a memory. Alejo de Rocas and his fiendish activities could be thrust firmly behind her.

Thank heaven he had nothing to do with the Centre. She had only worked there a short time, and she valued her job. The possibility that Alejo de Rocas might put in an appearance one day and make the connection between her and Luis did not bear thinking about.

CHAPTER TWO

'YOU are not eating, *señorita*. Is something wrong? Is the food not to your liking?'

'Oh, no, everything's fine, thank you.' Deanna stopped pushing the food around her plate and tried to reassure the waitress, answering her in the girl's native Spanish. 'I'm just not very hungry, that's all.'

Her appetite seemed to have disappeared, and she could only put it down to the events that had taken place in the afternoon. Now, in the cool confines of the hotel dining-room, she had ample time to reflect on the way things had gone. She hoped fervently that Luis was safe, that somehow Alejo de Rocas had been foiled.

Her own encounter with him had been thoroughly disturbing, her reactions to him confounding her so much that she wanted only to push it all to the back of her mind. His cool arrogance in manhandling her that way, as though he would do exactly as he pleased, set her teeth on edge.

Never before had she put herself into a situation where a man could take control; she had always been cautious, needing to stake out the boundaries to her own satisfaction.

Perhaps she was unusual in her attitude to relationships, but she could not share the light-hearted approach of her friends. At twenty-four, she knew she was something of an enigma to them, but her principles were too solidly ingrained for her to go back on them now.

Her upbringing must account for a lot, she supposed. The solid partnership of her parents, the obvious love that they shared, was a lasting example of what might be, and it was probably that which had made her spurn anything superficial. Their feelings for each other were strong and wholesome, and deep inside she held on to the hope that one day she might experience something similar.

Her mouth made a rueful, downward curve. For a long time, she had thought Richard might be the one for her. He had certainly made a deep impression on her, hadn't he, with his show of consideration and concern for her well-being when she had first begun to work for the pharmaceutical company in the Midlands? A director, paying her, a newcomer, so much personal attention—the whole thing had fazed her for quite a while—and then somehow the whole basis of their relationship had shifted.

How had it happened? Gradually her feelings had crystallised, become more clearly defined. She had come to believe that their companionship was a solid basis on which they could build something more enduring; that they could begin to share the deeper intimacy he was pressing her for. But that had been before she learned of the other woman in his life, the one who fulfilled all the needs that she had been more circumspect about.

Once again, she remembered with fond sadness, it had been Luis, paying one of his flying visits, who had shaken her out of her despondency.

'Come and work in Peru,' he had said. 'I know just the place that will suit you. My friend, Carmela, says they are desperate for someone to take on the organisational side of things at the distribution centre—medicines, health foods, all that kind of thing. With your knowledge of languages and your qualifications in business studies, you are just the person they are looking for.'

He had studied her thoughtfully, seeing the troubled hesitancy in her eyes. 'Why don't you give it a try? You have nothing to lose, and what is there for you here? You are not happy, and from what I can see there is little prospect of promotion within your department. Too many men climbing the ladder alongside you.'

What he had said had the ring of truth about it. And there was nothing to keep her in England. Her parents were constantly travelling, her aunts, uncles and cousins were scattered around various parts of the globe.

She was glad, now, that she had taken his advice. The move had been much more successful than she could ever have hoped. Now the only blot on her horizon was the fact that he was in trouble himself, and she was not able to do anything about it.

Sighing, she pushed away her plate. 'I'm sorry,' she said to the waitress. 'The food is delicious, I'm sure, but I'm a little weary, I think. It seems to have been a long day.'

'*Sí*. I will get coffee for you.' The girl began to clear away the dishes. 'The fiesta goes on for a long time, but it is a nice way to tire yourself, is it not?' She smiled. 'This is a special day, everyone should enjoy it. It is a great pity,' she added darkly, 'that Señor de Rocas did not join in with all the fun. Too much work is bad, very bad.'

Deanna shot her a wary, startled look. 'Señor de Rocas?' she queried.

The waitress slid a plate on to her tray. 'You know him, do you not? Everyone around here knows the name Rocas.'

'I've heard of him, of course,' Deanna said cautiously. 'Are you saying——? Is he here? In the hotel?'

'*Sí*.' Lifting the tray, the girl tossed back her glossy, raven hair. 'It is not anything new. He always takes a room here when he is back from his travels.'

'He does?' Deanna's voice took on a faint rasping sound, her pulse quickening to an erratic beat, as she assimilated the unpalatable truth.

The girl nodded. 'Most times. I like that. He is a very attractive man, you know.' She was lost in a reverie for a moment. 'But today is not good,' she said, getting back into her stride. 'He is in a foul mood, very bad-tempered.' Her hands wafted the air in a Latin gesture. 'No fiesta, you see.'

'You should learn to curb your tongue, Isabel.' The deeply glacial male tones cut through the air like a whiplash and the waitress stared in frank horror at a point beyond Deanna's chair. 'Go about your duties.' It was a harsh, implacable command.

Deanna's head snapped around, her eyes widening with shock. A silent wail grew inside her throat. He was in the hotel, the girl had said, but he shouldn't be here, not here at her table, before she'd even had time to gather breath. Perhaps he *was* the devil, as Luis claimed. He certainly carried with him a demonic infallibility for being in the wrong place at the wrong time. For her.

As Alejo de Rocas returned her gaze with cool deliberation, her mind raced into fifth gear. If he was as ill-tempered as Isabel suggested, it must mean that he had been thwarted, mustn't it? He couldn't know the true extent of her part in it, though, could he? He wouldn't have put two and two together and come up with the right answer. It wasn't possible, was it? But there was no casting aside the fact that here he was, standing within touching distance, and she didn't need a sage to tell her that he wasn't at all pleased to see her.

Isabel sniffed. 'I will bring coffee, Miss Sullivan.' Her brown eyes slid resentfully to Alejo de Rocas.

His expression was unyielding, austere. 'For two,' he said.

Deanna watched her walk away, her mind searching feverishly for a way out of a situation which, she was certain, could only bode trouble.

'You will not mind if I join you?' He addressed her coldly, already pulling out a chair, and she viewed him with arrant hostility.

'And if I do?'

His mouth curved in a smile, but there was nothing remotely friendly in the action.

'I see that your knowledge of the Spanish language has taken on a dramatic improvement since we last met. You are to be congratulated.' He seated himself at the table, his long, taut-muscled legs stretched out in a relaxed pose that didn't fool her for a minute. He was as tranquil as a coiled cobra.

'I'm a fast learner,' she informed him tartly. Her only defence was to attack, and she went at it, head-on. 'And I learned this afternoon that you are both arrogant and high-handed and that I don't at all care for your company.'

His sun-browned features were shaded in sardonic disregard. '*Calma*, Miss Sullivan,' he intoned drily. 'Let us at least preserve the civilities while we are in public view.'

'To what purpose?' she threw back with stinging vigour. 'I'd much prefer that you leave right now.'

'I've no doubt you would, but I have one or two questions to ask of you. A few explanations are in order, I believe.'

'You may believe whatever you wish. I see no reason to explain anything to you.'

'It does not stab your conscience that you implied you do not speak my language, when it is quite clear that you have an intimate knowledge of it?'

The gleaming curtain of her hair flickered across her face like a veil as she averted her gaze briefly. She hoped that he didn't see the quick flush of warmth that came to her cheeks. 'You were trying to move me from a place where I was happily settled. I felt no pressing need to do as you asked.'

'Were you not concerned that I needed to pass with my vehicle; that your action in obstructing me would cause me an unnecessary nuisance?'

She must have succeeded in keeping him from Luis. That was what lay behind his curt, frost-bitten interrogation. She hugged the thought close. 'The roads were closed to traffic,' she answered coolly. 'You could have backed up the way you had come, whereas I had every reason to be there with the flower cart.'

He smiled thinly. 'We will forget this pretence of a cart, Miss Sullivan. I judge you to have more intelligence than that. You were well aware of what you were doing.'

Her eyes narrowed smokily. 'I shall be happy to forget it. I shall be more than happy to forget you.'

'I doubt you will find that so easy.' He studied her thoughtfully, his dark eyes making a cool assessment that made her stiffen her spine. 'Where did you learn to speak Spanish so fluently?'

Watching Isabel approach with a tray of coffee, Deanna made up her mind to get away from him and his determined questioning at the first opportunity. 'At university, in England. I studied languages in conjunction with a business course.' Picking up her bag from the table, she added, 'Also, my father has been in the diplomatic service for many years. We travelled around a great deal, and I found I have something of an ear for language.'

Isabel placed the coffee-cups before them on the white cloth, and Deanna stood up, using the distraction of the girl's presence as a cover for her departure. 'My taste for coffee seems to have waned,' she informed him smoothly. 'You're welcome to it, *señor*. Please excuse me, I have things to do.'

She did not stay to witness his reaction. Walking swiftly away, she made for the wide staircase out in the foyer, and hurried up to her room, her narrow heels clicking on the marble floor. The sooner she reached the safety of her own domain, the better she would feel.

It was clear from his icily restrained demeanour that he was annoyed, that things had obviously not gone as he had expected this afternoon. That must mean that Luis had given him the slip, and she was heartily glad of that. If she had had any qualms earlier about the part she had played in the whole business, she had put them to rest now. The man was autocratic and disagreeable, and it was no wonder that Luis wanted to steer clear of him. He was the kind of man who expected everyone and everything to conform to his wishes, who was determined to get what he wanted, at whatever cost. He did not like it when things went wrong. Mistakes were obviously not written into his book of procedures.

His appearance in the hotel had alarmed her, but she had been worrying needlessly. Despite his remarks, he could not have guessed the real part she had played, could he? He was merely vexed because she had hindered him.

She rummaged in her bag for her key. Why did none of her arguments do anything to bring her reassurance? The man had a disconcerting tendency to slide under her carefully arranged composure, and tip it upside-down, that was the trouble. She had to scour him out of her mind, firmly and without any backsliding; it was the only answer. He had no place there.

Pushing open the door to her room, she stepped inside.

'*Gracias, señorita,*' Alejo de Rocas' deep voice sounded grittily in her ear. 'How kind of you to lead the way.'

Jerkily, Deanna swung round, the swift intake of her breath audible in the empty quiet of the first-floor corridor. 'What are you doing here?' she asked, the words sounding strained and thick. He had no business creeping up on her that way, silent as a black panther.

'Surely I did not mistake your intention, Miss Sullivan? You knew, of course, that this would be a much more comfortable place for us to continue our conversation.'

'You appear to have a somewhat overblown self-image,' she told him with caustic brevity. 'I'm afraid I have not the slightest inclination to spend time with you.'

She made to close the door on him, and found her hand covered by his own, the threatening pressure of his hard body forcing her back into the room.

'Regrets need be of no consequence, *señorita,*' he murmured silkily. 'I have more than enough enthusiasm for this meeting to carry both of us through it. Your behaviour this afternoon has been...shall we say...intriguing? Certainly, it seems to merit further investigation.'

Dry-mouthed, she absorbed the cynicism of his expression, tried desperately to ignore the strength inherent in the long fingers that clamped hers around the thick panelled edge of the door.

Looking down at those fingers, she said carefully, 'This is not the first time today that you have laid hands on me, Señor de Rocas. For your own sake, I sincerely hope that it's the last.'

'Then you must accede to my request, Miss Sullivan, and allow me the pleasure of your company.' Thrusting her backwards towards the centre of the room, he kicked the door shut behind him.

Deanna felt a tremor of alarm tighten the muscles of her stomach as he started towards her. Biting down on a shock-wave of apprehension, she queried stiffly, 'Is aggression yet another facet of your character that I have to contend with?' Scanning his sharply sculpted features, she was aware of the taut flick of muscle along the hard line of his jaw.

'I do not care for this—what is your term?' He paused, frowning. 'This...run-around. You have spent this afternoon playing out some game to your own satisfaction, pretending to be what you are not, and I should tell you, *señorita*, that where I would have been prepared to overlook an act of pure innocence I have no such intention now that I know what was truly in your mind.' His eyes narrowed. 'You have done your utmost to get in my way, and you have succeeded in what you set out to do. Your plans have all come to fruition; the bird has flown. Did you imagine there would be no reckoning to pay?' Again, that spasmodic tug of muscle. 'You were badly mistaken.'

Deanna moistened her lips faintly with the tip of her tongue. 'I really have no idea,' she said raggedly, 'what you are talking about.'

'*Es verdad*?' His brow rose in mocking disbelief. 'I think not. You must be very pleased with yourself. Your friend is well on his way by now, and it is all thanks to you.'

'My friend?' Her eyelids flickered, thick golden lashes sweeping downwards. 'I'm not sure that I follow this talk of flying birds. Are you sure you have the right person? Why should I have any interest whatsoever in you and your busy comings and goings? I think you're guilty of jumping to conclusions.' Delicately, she shrugged, one sun-flushed shoulder moving in lazy negligence. 'When I woke this morning, I had no thought in my head but to enjoy the fiesta.'

She felt the heat of his gaze moving over her in scintillating appreciation. 'What a pity you are not on the stage,' he murmured drily. 'You would make an excellent actress. Unfortunately, though, your talent is wasted on me. I prefer to concentrate my attention instead on discovering the whereabouts of Luis San Martin. A matter in which you can be of the greatest help.'

Swallowing against the taut constriction in her throat, Deanna let her fingers toy with the fine material of her skirt. 'What gives you that idea?'

'The fact that you were with him in this hotel, this very afternoon. He came with you to your room, and later you shared a drink with him on the private terrace by the pool.'

His mouth indented briefly at her startled gasp. 'I am well acquainted with the management,' he said. 'When I saw you in the dining-room a short while ago, it took only a few general enquiries to find out what I wanted to know. You left the hotel with him and went to the plaza, where, as we both know, you acted as his accomplice while he made his getaway.' His darkly brooding glance went to the wooden bedstead behind her. 'No doubt that was not the only favour you bestowed on him today.'

'How dare you?' Anger flared in her, her hand shooting out in sharp reaction to the insult, but he fielded it easily, catching her wrist in a powerful, controlled grasp.

'You will not add to your crimes by striking me, Deanna.' His voice had an abrasive, gravelled edge. 'Your touching final embrace on the terrace was a source of much conjecture. If you do not wish to start tongues wagging, you should do your kissing in private.'

She was stunned by the interpretation placed on such a brief hug and kiss between friends. 'You have——'

'It is of no account,' he cut in brusquely. 'I want to know where he is heading, and you will tell me.'

'Why should I?' she tossed back with cool indifference. 'Since you were careless enough to lose him in the first place, it appears to me that the problem is wholly yours. If you had him in your sights and you let him give you the slip, then you have only yourself to blame.'

His fingers tightened on her. 'There was an accident along the way. A truck in collision with a car.' His tone layered ice along her nerve-endings. 'You, I take it, would have me leave a man to bleed to his death at the roadside? Fortunately for him, I have my own code of ethics, and he is now being tended in the hospital.'

Deanna blinked back her shock at the carelessly thrown-out information. So Luis owed his escape to the calamity which had fallen on some other unhappy soul. She breathed in deeply.

'You assume too much,' she said tersely, offended by his brutal destruction of her character. 'What would you know of my feelings on the situation? And what business is it of yours where Luis chooses to go? What makes you think you can follow him about as you please, and scatter insults around me like so much confetti?' She ground her teeth. 'I don't like your manner, Señor de Rocas, and if you imagine that you can intimidate me in any way you're sadly mistaken. I will not be hounded; you're wasting your time, if you think I can be browbeaten. I will tell you nothing.' She spat the words at him, defiance sparking in her eyes, the fingers of her free hand clenching in the soft folds of her skirt.

His grip on her tightened, the muscles of his arm flexing beneath the black shirt as he drew her towards him. 'You throw out a challenge,' he intoned roughly, 'as though it might serve as some kind of deterrent to my plans. It does not. You cannot profit from this battle of wills, Deanna. Just the opposite, in fact. You are *intimately* acquainted with Luis San Martin, you have the key to what is in his head, and you will hand it over to me.'

'You're mistaken,' she told him in a strained tone, resenting the way he laid stress on the word. 'And even supposing that I had anything of worth to pass on, I would want to know much more of your intentions before I did so. Why are you so determined on pursuing him?'

His jaw clenched. 'This sham of innocence,' he said with slow precision, 'is fast losing its appeal. Could you not pursue some other course?'

'In all truth,' she persisted grittily, 'I don't know what reason you could have for wanting to follow Luis. Perhaps you would care to enlighten me?'

Scepticism scored his mouth. 'Play it how you will. At any rate, it is a private matter that I do not care to discuss. My only concern is to secure the details of his present whereabouts.'

Deanna sucked in another long breath. 'Then I'm afraid you will have a long wait.'

'So be it.' His eyes trailed a burning path over her slender form. 'I intend to win, you should know that, and crossing swords with a woman of spirit and fire simply makes the prospect of victory all the more satisfying. This is a skirmish which serves only to whet the appetite, and I shall have no great displeasure should it last the night through. The outcome will be still the same. Your stand against me is doomed to failure.'

She tugged sharply against his hold on her, recognising, as she did so, his greater strength and the futility of her actions. 'You will release me, *señor*. And I'll remind you once again that I don't respond to this...manhandling.'

'Do you not?' His soft, amused chuckle sent her temper shooting out of bounds, even as he let her go. Resisting the urge to rub away the tingling imprint of his fingers from her wrist, she moved away from him, backing up against the carved wooden dresser.

'Do you imagine,' she said, making a fierce effort to keep from him the cold well of nervousness that was surging inside her, 'that a show of force would make me divulge any dark secrets I might have? Think again, *señor*. The night may be long, but it's always followed by the dawn, and you may find that you have a reckoning of your own to pay. When the police arrive, you too will have a great deal of explaining to do.'

His mouth curved in a smile which did nothing to lessen her mounting tension. 'I am trembling at the mere thought of it,' he said with a deeply mocking inflexion. 'But perhaps it would be a price worth paying, if force were to my taste.'

His gleaming gaze flashed over her with disconcerting thoroughness, taking in her shapely curves, the rounded line of hip and thigh, coming back at length to rest on the warm pink of her cheeks. 'It is not, though. There are far better, more effective methods to hand, I believe, when dealing with a beautiful woman. I have the feeling that where coercion fails tender persuasion might reap its own reward.'

The stillness of the air was suddenly charged, a current flowing between them, tension vibrating in powerful waves through the quiet of the room. Deanna felt her flesh heat as the hot tide of her blood began to race wildly out of control, the throb of her heartbeat pounding heavily against her ribcage. Shifting, she edged even further backwards, pressing against the hard wood of the dresser.

He had not even needed to touch her for her senses to run riot, unruly imaginings mingling with fearful expectation. It took only one shimmering glance to create turmoil within her, to create in her a wild and reckless torment of emotion. Why should this man, a stranger, have such a profound effect on her, be able to storm her defences with such perfect ease?

'I can't think,' she said slowly, 'why you should want to waste energy on such a fruitless task.'

His dark eyes glittered in sensual appraisal. 'You try to discourage me,' he murmured, 'but it is not possible. There is more to be gained than mere information. Your golden English beauty tantalises me. You are a jewel, a treasure that any man would prize.'

'You should forget any ideas you may have on that score,' she said, feverishly conscious of her surroundings, the wooden bedstead, the inviting silk of its coverings. Her intense vulnerability was being driven home to her, more with each second that passed, and she was dismayed to find buried within herself some involuntary core of response, a fragmentary reaching out towards the dark attraction of his rugged masculinity. She must be going crazy; her hormones were obviously being sent haywire in this Peruvian climate.

'Alas,' he pronounced steadily, 'it is not within my nature to put aside something which I am set on. I am intrigued, enchanted by you, my lovely *Inglesa*, by your cool defiance.'

'I dare say rejection is something you haven't encountered before,' Deanna said in terse dismissal, all too conscious of his darkly attractive looks. In his early thirties, she guessed, he was devastatingly male, and he was probably used to women falling at his feet, to people rushing to obey his smallest bidding. 'You've pushed your way into my room, and I resent your presumption that you can do exactly as you wish. Be certain, Señor de Rocas, you have no power over me.'

'Alejo, please,' he said with soft insistence. 'My name is Alejo. If we are to become better acquainted, it is best you use it, I think.'

'Then you think wrongly, Señor de Rocas. I have learned quite sufficient about you already, and I wish you to leave. Now.'

'I am devastated by your cruelty,' he said, his eyes faintly gleaming. 'How could I possibly be induced to abandon the sweet promise of your affection?'

'I'm sure the management will play their part in that,' she retorted sharply. 'Despite your influence in the region, I've no doubt they will be forced to consider their own reputation. They would not, after all, care to have the matter made public.'

'What matter is this?' His mouth curved. 'I have done nothing... yet.' His gaze moved over her with a searching curiosity that increased her feelings of misgiving tenfold. 'And tell me, Deanna, how, precisely, do you intend to let them know?'

Her glance skittered to the telephone across the room. But how was she to get to it? Wedged as she was, between the bed and the dresser, with him in front of her, blocking her path, what was she to do? Could she force her way past him?

As though he had read her thoughts, his stance hardened, his long, tough frame an impenetrable barrier. 'A dilemma, is it not? Perhaps it would have been better had you thought of this before. It was *imprudente*—foolish in the extreme—to allow yourself to be closed in a room with a man you only met a few short hours ago. Do you know nothing of the Peruvian temperament? Our blood runs hot—*my* blood runs with the heat of the volcano; it burns for you.'

As he moved towards her, Deanna reacted with wary instinct, her spine pressing against the solid wood of the dresser, her arm encountering the polished surface. In desperation, she let her fingers travel jerkily towards the large china water jug.

'Then I had better do something, hadn't I,' she said in harassed tones, 'to extinguish the fire before it burns out of control?' Lifting the heavy vessel, she tilted it towards him.

His brow rose in astonishment. 'Do you imagine a little water will dampen my passion?' he queried with lazy interest, as he removed the pot from her fingers with insulting ease. 'What milksops have you entertained in your life before this?' Distaste curled his lips. Replacing the jug on its stand, he said thoughtfully, 'You will discover, *enamorada*, that I am not to be so readily diverted.'

He reached for her hand, his thumb stroking gently along her palm. The slow, feathering action sent fiery signals along her nerve pathways, sparking her senses into flaming discord, at war with the clutch of apprehension that knotted her stomach.

'I really don't think I care to make any more discoveries about you, *señor*,' she said, striving to keep her voice even. 'I want you to leave this room. I want you to go, now.'

'But that would be such a waste,' he murmured, his accent thickening as he turned her hand in his, the gliding motion of his thumb continuing. 'And there is so much to be gained by staying.' His glance travelled over her, taking in the faint flush of her cheeks, lingering on the full pink curve of her mouth. She prayed that he did not see its betraying quiver.

'I have ordered a late-night drink to be brought to my room,' she lied casually. 'When the waitress arrives, you will have no choice but to do as I ask... if you value your standing in society.'

A glinting appreciation flickered momentarily in his eyes. 'I have frightened you,' he said, his Spanish heritage evident in his dark gaze. 'That was not my intention. I apologise. I had meant to teach you a lesson, and I think I have succeeded in that. Let me make amends, Deanna. I will show you that I am not an ogre to be feared.'

He looked over to the low couch that rested against the far wall. 'Come, shall we not make ourselves comfortable? You could tell me about yourself, help me to know all there is to know about you. Are you *turista*? How long will you be in Peru?'

The knot twisted inside her. It was a ploy. He had seen through her fragile artifice, and he had no intention of leaving. Tiny beads of perspiration pearled on her forehead. There had to be a way to get him out of here. His presence was far too dangerous to her peace of mind.

Luis had been right all along. Alejo de Rocas was the devil incarnate, determined on a path from which he would not be swayed. He wanted information, and he did not care how he obtained it.

All right, then, she would feed him what he wanted. By the time he discovered that he had been duped, she would be well away from here.

'I shall be comfortable enough once you've gone,' she told him stiffly. 'I've no desire to prolong this conversation and I don't believe that it is me who interests you. You came here because you wanted to know about Luis and I told you that I know nothing. That was true. Or——' she felt him move impatiently '—at least it was mostly true. I know very little about what's going on.'

His firm mouth quirked in a way that signified indifference. 'We have been through this,' he said. 'I do not wish to travel the same boards twice. Besides,' his voice lowered to a caressing, throbbing murmur, 'you are wrong in discounting my interest in you. You have distracted me, you have aroused my curiosity, and Luis is but a shadow in my mind now. It is you I want to know about.'

His fingers lightly trailed the silken length of her arm, and she absorbed the sensation with tremulous fascination. 'Sit with me, Deanna,' he urged softly. 'This afternoon we met only briefly, but even then I was drawn to find out more about you. Now, since my journey came to nothing, I find I am in no great hurry, and we have all the time in the world to get to know each other.'

Shifting evasively, she twisted away from the gentle pressure of his hand on her arm. 'I don't think that sitting with you would be a good idea. Earlier,' she reminded him, 'you were determined on finding Luis. I didn't understand why, and I thought you might mean to harm him—but perhaps I made a mistake in that.' She hesitated. 'I wonder if I should tell you the little that I know? If it will persuade you to go...' She let it seem as though she was mulling things over. 'You're a man of power and authority in these parts, but it would hardly enhance your reputation if you were seen to be acting in a harsh and unreasonable manner, would it? Far better if you dealt with the dispute between you both in a way that is scrupulously fair.'

Her gaze fixed on him questioningly. 'Can I trust you to see that he is treated well; that you'll listen to his side of things?'

The taut planes of his face were shaded as he studied her; she could not read the expression behind his eyes. 'You have my word,' he said, 'that San Martin will be treated as he deserves. However, if you have no idea of his whereabouts, the matter is immaterial, *sin importancia*. Is that not so?'

'I may be able to help—in some small way. It's just guesswork, though, nothing substantial, you understand?' She looked at him, and he waited, the sleek panther staring with unblinking gaze.

'There's a chance,' she went on hurriedly, 'that he may be heading north. He has relatives, in Calcara.' At least that bit was true, she excused herself. 'I think it's possible he may have gone to them. They have a small cottage close by the hacienda.'

He regarded her shrewdly. 'I hope,' he said deeply, 'that what you are telling me is the truth. I should not like to have another wasted journey.'

She tried on a weak smile. 'Of course not,' she muttered. 'Would I send you on a false mission, when you've given me your word?'

His eyes glittered. 'I should say that was more than a possibility. But it will avail you nothing, in the end. In the meantime, I will, regretfully, take my leave of you, *enamorada*. You will miss me, no?' His mouth made a sardonic twist at her restrained silence, and he began to walk across the room.

At the door, he paused. '*Pase lo que pase*,' he murmured. 'Come what may—I shall return, Deanna. Be sure of that.'

She let out a long, pent-up breath as the door closed behind him. Return as he might, he would not find her here. The journey to Calcara was long and tedious, and by the time he came back, empty-handed, she would be on her way to the Centre, and back to normality.

CHAPTER THREE

'I *AM* very sorry, *señorita*. The festival has caused much delay, and the spare parts we needed have not yet arrived. Perhaps if you come back tomorrow, or the day after, we shall have fixed the truck.'

Deanna's spirits plummeted as the mechanic gave her a grimacing look of apology, his shoulders moving in a fatalistic shrug. '*Mañana*,' he said helpfully. 'Try again then.'

'*Mañana* will be too late,' she muttered distractedly. There was no way she could stay any longer in this town. The prospect didn't bear thinking about, not with Alejo de Rocas setting out hotfoot from Calcara. She had no doubt that vengeance would spur him to track her down the minute he arrived back here, and it was imperative she make a fast disappearing act. It had been her first thought this morning, to get away as early as humanly possible.

Only, things were decidedly not going as planned. Waiting around while the mechanic had sifted through his paperwork and made various calls had made her much later than she had intended in starting out for the Centre. And it had all been for nothing in the end. Still the truck was not ready.

'I can't wait,' she said in frustration. 'I have to get back to work. Couldn't you arrange for its delivery to me just as soon as it has been fixed?' It would cost her more that way, but there was little she could do about it, and anyway, it was more than likely that staying over another night at the hotel would prove even more expensive.

'No problem, I will see to it,' the man said, and she had to be content to leave it at that. Emerging from the dark, untidy office of the garage on to the street, she was relieved to exchange the reek of oil and petroleum for the fresh, flower-scented air outside.

If she hadn't been in such a hurry, it would have been an even greater pleasure to wander along the avenues and peer in at the shops, with their wealth of pottery and jewelled craftwork. Snatches of song, remnants of the fiesta, not yet forgotten, drifted out from various open doorways as she walked along. The warm, balmy atmosphere was soothing; she could even have made a few small purchases.

She pushed her purse firmly into the pocket of her light cotton jacket. Another time. Right now, she had to sort out her travel arrangements. Trucks regularly made the journey into the valley, she recalled, and it was not unusual for people to use them as a mode of transport. All she had to do was find the depot.

Glancing along the busy street as she walked towards the imposing façade of the hotel, her gaze made a sudden ricochet, her steps faltering. The now familiar lithe, dark figure of a man was coming steadily into view.

Her fingertips dug tightly into her palms. Lord, he must have completed his journey in double-quick time. Why was this happening to her? Why had an innocuous visit to a small town turned out to be so full of complications? There had to be some way she could get away from him.

Just as she considered her escape route, a small child ran full tilt along the street, his little face intent, and even from this distance she could see the glitter of tears as they trickled down his cheeks. He couldn't be more than about three or four years old, and it looked as though he was alone and lost.

'*Mamá*,' he cried, '*Mamá*!' bewilderment crumpling his pinched features as he paused like a shaky raft in the midst of a swirling sea of people. Deanna started towards him, wondering if his mother was in one of the shops near by, and then she stopped abruptly as she saw Alejo de Rocas kneeling down beside the child.

His hands were gentle around the thin little shoulders, and it was clear that he was talking softly to the boy in a way that was obviously soothing, as the tears slowly came to an end, and a grubby little fist knuckled them away. Deanna felt a painful dryness form in her throat as she watched them together. Lifting the child, Alejo held him up, safe and secure in his arms, above the crowd, and with a joyful shout the toddler began to wave his hands in the air. '*Mamá*,' he called again. His frantic mother pushed her way through the mass of people, the worry that was etched on her face smoothing out as she came to Alejo. He handed over the boy with a few commiserating words, then glanced once more along the avenue.

Preoccupied, Deanna had just a moment to glimpse the changing set of his mouth before she recollected the impending hazards of her own situation, and shot rapidly into a quiet side-street. Her heart was pounding as she hurried by the tall buildings. Had he seen her? She quickened her pace.

'So, Miss Sullivan——' Alejo de Rocas bore down on her, taut menace shadowing the sharply honed lines of his face '—we meet again.'

He must have moved like lightning. Her jaw worked in an involuntary spasm and he caught her hunted look with grim satisfaction. 'Had you thought to avoid me a second time?' he gritted, his voice gravelly, deep, rippling with cool fingers along her nervous system. 'A wasted hope, my beautiful, treacherous deceiver. I warned you that I would return, did I not?'

She stiffened, making herself face him squarely, arching a finely shaped brow. 'Am I to take it from your hostile tone that you've been unsuccessful yet again? This is becoming something of a habit, *señor*.'

'Isn't it? It is what comes of listening to the words of a dark angel, the price one pays for trusting in sweet moonshine. You sent me on a fool's errand, used me as a focus for your trickery once more.'

'You're maligning me,' she hit back with bracing verve. 'What I told you was the truth. Luis's relatives have always lived in Calcara. It's hardly my fault if they don't know where he is at this moment.'

'I am not to be led into that mist of falsehoods a second time,' he pronounced impatiently, his voice rough with a Spanish burr. 'These relatives are a figment of your imagination, your so lively world of pure fantasy and fabulous myth.'

Her head went back at that, her blue eyes scanning him with smouldering intensity. 'I see you are your usual boorish self again. The problem of finding Luis San Martin is all yours, Señor de Rocas. Clearly, I can be of no help to you, and I do have other things to attend to.'

She would not let herself be rattled by him. In doing what she could to help Luis, she was submerging herself deeper and deeper in trouble, and it had to end. If she was to get her life back on to an even keel once more, she had to shrug off this man and get on with things as she had intended at the start of the morning. She would go back to the hotel and pick up the medical supplies she had collected earlier.

As she started to move briskly away, he sidestepped her. 'Where do you think you are going?'

'Anywhere, as long as it's far away from you,' she informed him tartly. 'Why should I stay and listen to your invective, just because you can't find a perfectly ordinary cottage that a blind man would locate in the shake of a dog's tail?'

Again, she made to walk away, and he went with her, his hands coming out to grip her shoulders, forcing her to remain still, to acknowledge him. The heat and pressure of his touch scorched through the thin covering of her jacket, firing off feverish alarm signals, her body reacting in startled, bitter awareness. She stared up at him, storm clouds gathering in her eyes. 'I wish to leave,' she reminded him with fierce resolution.

'But you will stay, my lovely cheat,' he intoned thickly, 'because I have not yet finished with you, not by a long way.' His burning glance shot over her, like wildfire, the heat of it streaking through her veins like flame. 'I am not to be duped yet again by that look of chaste innocence, nor to be thrown by that cool, haughty demeanour. You think you can protect your lover by stringing me a false line, but I am here to rid you of that idea once and for all.'

His dark eyes studied her broodingly, sliding down, more slowly this time, over the cotton suit she wore, tracing the line of the blouson jacket, nipped in at her slender waist and flaring out over smoothly rounded hips, the skirt faithfully hugging her curving figure. 'I could almost,' he said roughly, 'find it in me to envy San Martin the loyalty you show him.' His grip on her tightened. 'Almost, but not quite. You would do anything for your handsome lover, would you not?'

'You're jumping to conclusions, *señor*,' she informed him coldly, stung by the raw violence in his tone. 'It appears to be a fault you have, this leaping in with assumptions and bandying them around as though they have some basis in reality.' She flicked back her head in a quick gesture of dismissal, the golden waves of her hair tumbling in shining disarray around her shoulders. 'There's nothing more I can do to help you in your search. His relatives might have been able to come up with something, but I've given you the only reliable information I have—the whereabouts of the cottage.'

The hard line of his mouth took on a cynical slant. 'This cottage, which has been boarded up for months—there is scant faith to be placed in such information, you will agree?'

She frowned, puzzlement in her glance. 'Boarded up? I didn't know that. Are you quite sure——?'

'Perfectly,' he cut in, with scalding contempt. 'Everything was exactly as you might have expected, all part of the complicity deployed by you and your devious boyfriend. Another exercise in time-wasting, to keep me from following his trail.'

'I had no idea that the cottage has been abandoned,' she said in sharp defence, alarmed by the undercurrent of savagery that threaded his voice. 'It belonged to one of his uncles, and I thought he was still living there.'

'But you knew,' Alejo de Rocas said with brittle emphasis, 'that Luis San Martin would have gone nowhere near it.'

'Did I?' The forced casualness of her tone belied her inner qualms at his faultless perception. She was disturbingly aware of her increasing vulnerability to this hard-edged man, vibrantly conscious of the hands firmly gripping her arms. 'You seem to credit me with an almost total insight into the workings of his mind. I don't have that, but I do know that he wouldn't have done anything to deserve this persecution, this witch hunt. He has my complete and unfailing trust.'

Her tormentor's mouth made a hard, slashing line, and a sudden shiver ran through her. The fact that they were standing out in the open, in full daylight, in a street, did nothing to allay her fears.

'Your rush to defend him is both misguided and revealing,' he remarked. 'Revealing in more ways than one. I see that he has spoken to you, after all; that you are not in complete ignorance of the situation, as you claimed.' His piercing eyes lanced her, the dark speculation in his swift appraisal unnerving. 'You should forget your devotion to this worthless lover,' he instructed her harshly. 'He leaves you to fight his battles, to face the devil alone, and pay his price. What kind of man is he, who would do that, who would involve you in his black deeds?'

'He hasn't done that,' she said in quick denial, twisting away from him and guardedly watching his frowning reaction. 'You're the one without scruples,' she accused him. 'You're intent only on getting what you want, and you wouldn't think twice about sacrificing me along the way. Well, don't expect me to sit around and wait to become your next victim. My sense of self-preservation is far too lively to allow me to fall into that trap.' Moving swiftly, she hurried towards the main thoroughfare, thankful to be back among the jostling crowd once more.

'Safety in numbers? Is that what you think?' His voice was a low growl in her ear.

'Luis is a good man, and you are hounding him, that is what I think,' she responded fiercely. 'And I've spent enough time answering your questions. There's nothing more I have to say to you.'

She swivelled away from him, and at that moment a man collided with her, stopped in his headlong rush as she stepped into his path. Reeling backwards, she was steadied only by Alejo's hand at her waist.

'Are you hurt?' he demanded, a line etched into his brow as he shot a narrowed glance after the man who was now disappearing into the mass of shoppers.

'No, no, I'm all right,' she answered him a little shakily. 'Thank you.' Drawing back, she said, 'I have to go, I've delayed long enough.'

'You are going back to the hotel?'

She did not want to answer him, to let him know where she was headed, but his slow half-smile signalled his recognition of the reasoning behind her hesitation.

'If I want to find you, Deanna, trust in me, I shall do so.'

Somehow, she did not doubt it. He was a man of influence, and it was a black cloud looming on her horizon that he would never give up his quest for Luis. While he believed she held the answer to where he had gone, he would continue to pursue her, no matter where she went.

'I hope you don't expect me to keep you informed. I'm not in the habit of issuing itineraries.' She reached in her pocket for her purse. She would need it at the truck depot, if she were to book her transport.

'Then I shall not make the mistake of asking again,' he said, amusement threading his voice. His features darkened as he saw her panicked expression. 'What is wrong?'

'My purse,' she said in frantic confusion. 'My purse has gone.' In growing agitation, she glanced along the pavement. 'I couldn't have dropped it, I only had it a few moments ago. I remember checking it.'

People milled around them, throwing out curious glances as she continued to search. 'I know I had it in my pocket,' she said, frustration edging her voice.

'It is possible,' Alejo said, 'that the man who pushed by you did not do so without purpose.'

Deanna stared at him unhappily. 'The man in the yellow shirt—do you mean that he might have taken it? I just didn't think—I was distracted; if I'd been paying more attention, instead of arguing with you—oh, this is terrible,' she muttered, voicing her thoughts aloud in a ragged undertone. 'How am I going to get home? How am I to pay the truck driver?'

She turned and scanned the street, absently answering the queries of interested passers-by. There was a lot of expressive lifting of shoulders and hands, and there were many murmurs of sympathy, but it seemed that her purse was well and truly lost. She could only hope that the truck driver, when she eventually found one, would wait for his money until she arrived back at the Centre.

Turning back to speak to Alejo once more, she was stunned to realise that he was no longer there. A quick survey beyond the huddle of shoppers revealed that he was nowhere to be seen, and somehow the knowledge that he had walked away without a word had a deeply unsettling effect on her. She had not known him for long, yet his action in leaving her seemed so out of character. Perhaps he had lost interest, she thought with faint bitterness, once it appeared that she had problems of her own, and that there was little more to be gained from continuing his inquisition.

At least his departure put an end to one of her troubles. She should have been filled with relief, shouldn't she? Not...what was it that she felt? Disappointment? Surely not? This feeling of deflation was unnatural, it had to be; it was something she simply could not explain.

A sigh hovered on her lips. This whole trip was turning out to be a complete disaster. All she needed now was to discover that there was no truck going her way today.

'Would you put in a call for me, please, to the Lakuno Distribution Centre?' Standing in front of the reception desk at the hotel while the girl dialled the number, Deanna was forced to concede that her bleak prediction had turned out to be woefully accurate. She stared despondently across the foyer, only to stiffen in wondering surprise as Alejo walked in through the wide, colonnaded entrance.

'From your doleful expression,' he said, 'it would seem that your travel plans have come to nothing. What happened, Deanna *mia*—did you discover that trucks only go through Lakuno on three days a week?'

So he had heard her muttered ramblings. Was there nothing he missed, nothing he did not know about? 'And this is not one of those days,' she agreed ruefully. 'Yes, you're quite right. It's what I might have expected, considering the way things have been turning out up to now.' She sent him a questioning look, a faint quiver of unease shifting through her. 'How did you know that I was going to Lakuno?'

A transient gleam flickered in his eyes. 'Did I not say that I would find you? When you know me better, *enamorada*, you will come to realise that I do not make idle talk.' His lips made a wry twist. 'It was no great feat, however. When I arrived here earlier, the receptionist was busy putting away your packages. I could not help but notice the address stamped on them.'

He laughed at her vexed expression. 'I have spoiled your secret. I am so sorry. You must forgive me.'

His patent enjoyment of her discomfiture annoyed her even more. This man would never give up. He had an obstinate streak a mile wide, she decided irritably. Persistence must be his middle name. She bit back a sigh at her own perversity. The very ambivalence of her emotions made her uncomfortable with herself. When she thought he had left her in the street, the sensations she had experienced had been baffling; she had gone through a feeling of let-down, of disillusionment, almost. Yet now he was back, here she was, hackles rising, prickly as a cat again.

'I thought you'd gone,' she said. 'You disappeared, and I didn't expect to see you again. I was thankful,' she stressed heavily, to emphasise the point, 'because I hoped that would be the last of your inquisition and tiresome pursuit.'

'Such a negative outlook,' he murmured, completely unperturbed, and she pressed her lips firmly together. 'I had hoped,' he said, 'that I might catch up with the man who took your purse. Unfortunately, the delay was too great, and he managed to slip away temporarily. We shall not worry, though. I have spoken to the *policía*, and they will continue the search.'

'I...thank you. It was kind of you to go to so much trouble.'

He nodded perfunctorily. 'It is a sad fact that, these days, one must be extra-vigilant with one's property.'

Just then, the receptionist interrupted in apologetic tones, the telephone receiver in her hand. 'There is no reply,' she said to Deanna. 'I'm afraid I cannot put the call through for you—no one is answering.'

Deanna thanked the girl, and abstractedly drummed her fingertips on the counter. Carmela must be away, and that meant her last option was used up, since it seemed there was no one at the Centre who could come out here and pick her up. The number of brick walls she kept coming up against was beginning to be depressing.

'I wonder,' she asked the girl, 'if I could book my room for a further night?' By tomorrow,

Carmela would be back, and her problems would be solved.

'The room you were staying in has already been let to someone else, Miss Sullivan, since you had said you were leaving today. We could, though, offer you another one, but you will need to pay in advance, to secure it, as you did before.'

Deanna looked at her doubtfully. 'Yes—I realise that's the way things are done, but you see, my purse was stolen this morning, and I can't pay right away—I have money in Lakuno, though, and as soon as I can contact my friend she'll drive over here and we can straighten everything out then.'

The receptionist shook her head, frowning. 'I am sorry, but we must have money in advance. It is a management rule, and I dare not break it. We have had problems in the past, you know, because, unhappily, everyone is not honest.'

'But—in the circumstances—could you not waive it this once?'

'It is not possible.' The girl's brows drew together, and then, glancing across at Deanna's tall, silently observing companion, she added, 'Unless, of course, Señor de Rocas would vouch for you?'

Deanna felt her heart quicken. Would he do that? Would he help her, after she had done her best to obstruct him? She swallowed painfully. It was not something she could pin her hopes on.

His glance ran over her. 'I do not think that remedy will serve.' With all the cold authority of his aristocratic ancestry, he confirmed her misgivings.

Miserably, she tried not to let her despair show. She had foreseen his shattering refusal, and she would not add to her humiliation by pleading with him to change his mind. It was her own fault for continually thwarting him. Who could blame him if now he sought to turn the tables on her?

'I suppose,' she muttered vaguely, searching her mind for a solution, 'I shall have to inform the police of my situation.' Though what answer they might give did not spring readily to mind. 'Perhaps you would have my packages stacked by the entrance,' she said to the girl. 'I'll make some arrangements to have them removed.' Quite what she would do she wasn't exactly sure.

'Have them deposited in my vehicle,' Alejo said. 'The Rocas plantation is on the way to Lakuno. You will travel with me, Deanna.'

'Go with you?' She was thrown into confusion by his peremptory decision, which had overturned all her preconceived ideas. 'But I thought——' She broke off, stumbling to a halt.

His brow rose. 'You thought—what?'

She felt the heat in her cheeks. 'Nothing. I am in your debt. Thank you.'

'*Está bien*. We will start out as soon as your parcels have been loaded.' He checked the gold watch on his wrist. 'We should arrive in time for the evening meal. You will sample the fruit of the Rocas plantation and let me know your opinion. It is the finest, I think.'

'The—the plantation?' Uncertainty threaded her voice. 'But I assumed—I must have misunderstood, but I thought you had meant to go to Lakuno.'

'And so we shall.' He led her out of the hotel towards the car park, his hand resting lightly against the small of her back. Relief mingled with the wild sensation evoked by that casual touch.

The boxes were stowed compactly in the Range Rover, she noted, and as he held open the door for her she slid carefully into the passenger seat. He started the vehicle into purring motion, and she tried to relax, conscious all the time of his proximity, recognising his competent hand at the wheel.

'How far is the plantation from Lakuno?' she asked, once they were easing around the tree-clad slopes of the Andean foothills, following a precipitous, curving route towards the lush green valley below.

'An hour or so,' he murmured. 'Not too long a journey in daylight. But as night draws in it will be increasingly hazardous to travel these roads, you agree?'

He glanced at her obliquely, and unwilling comprehension skittered across her mind, the true extent of her folly slowly beginning to dawn on her. 'Señor de Rocas——'

'Alejo,' he reminded her. 'We have had this conversation before, have we not?'

She breathed in deeply to still her throbbing pulse. 'Alejo,' she yielded fractionally, trying to ignore his slow smile of satisfaction. 'When, exactly, will we be arriving at Lakuno?'

He appeared to give it some thought. 'It is difficult to be precise, you understand? But I had considered that some time not too distant from lunch tomorrow might be a pleasing arrangement.'

'Pleasing?' She struggled to keep her voice steady. 'I'd rather hoped that tonight——'

'Tonight,' he interrupted smoothly, 'you will, of course, be my guest.'

CHAPTER FOUR

'You are scowling, *enamorada*,' Alejo said as he parked the Range Rover in front of a large Spanish colonial-style mansion. 'Do I take it that you are still not reconciled to spending the night with me?'

His tone mocked her and she glowered even more as she stepped down from the vehicle. His words had undercurrents of sensual meaning that created a riptide of warring emotions to rage within her. Did he know how unsettled he made her feel? Of course he did.

She must at all costs keep a clamp on her turbulent imaginings, hide her reactions to his powerful masculinity, or she would be lost. A man like Alejo de Rocas must be well aware of his effect on women, but she could not afford to let herself fall into his baited trap. She had just spent several hours with him, with barely a hair's breadth between them, and it had not eased her tension in the slightest. He was incredibly good-looking, a virile, superbly male individual, and the thoughts evoked by his casual words stirred in her feelings that she would much rather had remained dormant.

This man was her enemy, she reminded herself; they were on opposite sides. He was only intent on getting to Luis, and it was clear that he had no compunction in using her to clear his path. If a little dalliance added spice to his journey, as far as he was concerned, that was all the better.

She had to be strong, refuse to be caught up in the silken bonds he was slowly weaving around her.

'I'm not amused by your cheap jests,' she retorted briskly, stretching limbs that had been stiffened by the long journey. 'You tricked me. You knew very well that I would never have come along with you had I known that you planned this overnight stop. I would have explained my situation to the police and let them help.'

'You would not have found their hostel accommodation to your liking,' he said firmly. 'Besides, what reason have you to fuss at the way things are turning out? Think of the positive aspect. If your purse is retrieved, it will be brought to me. Who knows? By morning you may have it once more in your possession.'

She was not appeased. He had brought her here under false pretences, and she did not trust him one inch. Alarm signals had been sounding off inside her throughout this whole trip, and she was beginning to feel the strain of it. Running a hand through the tangled mass of her hair, she reflected wretchedly that she was hot and thirsty, and that she must look as untidy as she felt.

His dark gaze raked her. 'You are weary,' he said. 'These roads are not the most comfortable to travel, but you will feel much better after a shower, and something to eat. Come. Let us go into the house.'

Was he always so intuitive? Trust him or not, she could not fault his show of consideration so far. Whatever his motives, she had to recognise that when she had been at her lowest ebb he had stepped in and offered her an alternative solution. She had been vulnerable and had seized it with both hands, and she had only herself to blame if, at this late stage, she had begun to question the wisdom of her actions.

'I'm being ungrateful,' she muttered. 'I apologise. I am, of course, thankful for your help. It's just that everything has gone wrong today—these last few days—and I'm thoroughly out of sorts.' She paused, taking stock of her surroundings once more, recalling the acres of land they had passed through to reach this place. 'Your plantation is more vast than I ever imagined,' she told him truthfully, her glance coming to dwell on the lush slopes that stretched far into the distance. Lit by the glow of the setting sun, the carefully tended terraces radiated brilliant colour.

'Mostly, we grow pineapples and lemons,' Alejo told her, surveying the spreading crops. 'But there are orange groves also. It is important to diversify, and I have other land, further north, where we grow papaws, avocados, aguapa, and suchlike.'

'I'm impressed,' she murmured. 'I've never seen anything like it, on such a scale. This isn't just marketed locally, is it?'

He laughed. 'You are quite right,' he said, leading the way to the white-painted house and showing her into the cool, spacious hallway. Large brass planters were filled with spreading green foliage, huge flower arrangements on ornate white marble stands filled the air with their scent. She breathed in appreciatively.

'Much of the fruit is sent to my canning factories,' he explained as he walked with her towards a wide, sweeping staircase. 'And we have a thriving international export market. There are Rocas company offices in the capitals of Europe, as well as in the States.'

'You've just returned from there?'

Abruptly, his jaw clenched. 'I see that San Martin has kept you well advised.'

Deanna shrugged. 'Perhaps. But Isabel said that you had just come back from your travels.'

Still frowning, he started up the stairs, indicating that she should follow. 'I have ordered that a room be prepared for you,' he said, coolly polite. 'I rang from the hotel to ensure that your needs are catered for, but if there is anything further that you require my housekeeper will be happy to assist you.'

He pushed open the door to a sumptuously furnished room, lavishly upholstered in pale rose-coloured silks, the thick-piled carpet a blend of deeper shades, the velvet drapes carefully arranged in an elegant, curving flow to skirt the floor.

'The bell-pull is by the bed, should you wish for attention,' he advised her with formal courtesy. 'I shall leave you for now. Dinner will be in one hour.'

Left alone, Deanna contemplated his return to cold displeasure. He did not like her connections with Luis, her part in his defection still angered him, and he would do whatever was necessary to uncover the truth. It was a timely warning, a sinister reminder, if she needed one, of the real reason behind her presence in his home.

Her luggage arrived while she was in the shower, and, wrapping herself in a towelling robe, she searched through it, taking out a cool, prettily styled dress. The delicate print, with its heart-shaped neckline and fitted bodice, fell in soft folds over the flare of her hips. It was one of her favourites, and it gave her a little confidence to wear it. Blow-drying her hair, she brushed it into shining waves, then added a final touch of perfume to her pulse-points before starting downstairs.

Alejo met her in the hall. '*Bueno*,' he said, his glance slanting over her briefly, his expression dark and unreadable. 'I see that you are punctual. Let us go and eat.' Showing her into a panelled dining-room, he added, 'I hope you will like our food—Rosana has prepared for us a Creole dish with chilli peppers, but if that is not to your taste there is a delicious seafood dish, made with *langostinos* and *limón*.'

Deanna had nothing but admiration for the unseen Rosana. 'This must rank as the best meal I've ever tasted,' she told Alejo with unqualified enthusiasm some time later. Scooping a last mouthful of *chirimoya*, she let it dissolve on her tongue, and then licked the sweet flavour delicately from her lips.

'It is good to see such enjoyment,' he answered, watching the action, his gaze moving with slow deliberation over the moist curve of her mouth. 'You must try our *pisco sour*. If you have a sweet tooth, you will like it, I am sure. It is a grape brandy, with nutmeg and egg-white, a truly potent combination.'

'Potent?' she queried, as he handed her a measure of the liquid.

His smile was a mixture of intrigue and invitation, dangerously bone-melting. 'Try it,' he urged in soft persuasion. 'One, or even two glasses—what peril lies in that?'

Her gaze narrowed on him as she took her first sip. A clear head was what she needed, wasn't it? She sensed a duel, a call to arms threatening in the hazy distance, and the stakes would be high, very high. Winner take all. She blinked, her lashes flickering briefly to dust her cheeks, the burn in her throat a powerful warning.

'What foundation is there for your apprehension?' he murmured lightly, accurately interpreting her inner thoughts once more. 'If the worst comes to the worst, I am here to put you to bed, after all. It will be my pleasure, have no doubt.'

She bared her teeth. 'Don't deceive yourself, will you? I hold my drink well, and if I have to defend my honour I can tell you I will bite and scratch, and the devil will come off worst.'

Soft laughter rumbled in his throat. 'So, the kitten has claws, and she is not afraid to use them. I like that, *gatita*. I like that very much. You amuse me with your quaint talk of honour; it fills me with thoughts of all those things that go along with it, like victory and conquest, and the spoils of war.'

'I think,' she stated firmly, putting down the empty glass, 'your downfall is yet to come. You had better take extra care.'

'I will do that, Deanna,' he agreed readily enough. 'Especially when I am planning my strategy around you.'

A line furrowed its way into her brow, and she watched him slowly pour out more brandy. His eyes glinted as he held out the crystal goblet to her.

'Bring your drink with you,' he said. 'I will show you my collection of Peruvian art. I think you will appreciate it.'

Still not sure precisely who had won that battle of wills, she went with him to an ante-room, where glass-fronted cases housed what must be a priceless assortment of pottery and jewelled relics.

She stared in silence for a moment at the sheer splendour of it, her pupils dilated with wonder. Then, 'It's incredible,' she breathed. 'It's so unbelievable that all these fantastic objects should be here, in one place, owned by one man.' She pressed her fingertips lightly to the glass. 'Surely those date back to almost 400BC? Aren't they part of the ancient Chavin culture? That reddish-brown colouring, the cylindrical neck—and that——' she moved on to the next case '—that's a Chimu ceremonial knife, isn't it? It's so beautiful; just look at those emeralds embedded in the hilt.'

'Yes, you are quite right. And these gold vessels too are ceremonial. For purely utilitarian purposes, bronze was used.'

He walked towards the next case, and said, 'These artefacts you will probably recognise as pre-Hispanic. They are not made from precious metals, being only of clay, but their interest lies elsewhere, would you not agree?'

She followed him, peering in at the contents. 'Oh.' Drawing back a little, she struggled to adjust her features to hide the quick flood of embarrassment that swept through her. 'I can't say,' she said slowly, 'that they hold a great deal of interest for me.'

His mouth twisted. 'It was a culture absorbed in its own eroticism.'

'A culture that has been dead for many centuries,' she pointed out, still trying to gain her composure.

'But which lives on in its pottery.' He drew her away to look at a less controversial array of turquoise jewellery. 'You appear well informed on many of the pieces,' he remarked. 'It is my turn to be impressed. I wonder, though, who imparted this knowledge to you? It was not part of your studies, I believe, but those of your dear friend, Luis San Martin. You must have worked closely together in order for you to learn so much.'

The curt edge to his voice made her cautious. 'Not so much,' she denied. 'I've always been fascinated by this kind of thing, but it's Luis who chose to make it his career, not I.'

'You knew, then, that he was cataloguing my collection?'

Warily, she nodded. 'He told me.'

'And he must also have told you why he was leaving, and where he was going at such short notice.'

Her mouth set in an obstinate line. 'That's not true, and I'm getting tired of repeating myself. You may believe whatever you wish.'

'Then I would have you know,' he said in a low drawl, 'that it is my firm belief that Luis would not leave behind such a precious possession as yourself for any longer than is absolutely necessary. Sooner or later, he will make contact with you.'

She looked at him steadily. 'I think I'm beginning to see what your plan is. How slow of me not to have worked it out sooner. Are you intent on shadowing my every move until he gets in touch? I wonder if you realise just how many months distant that contact might be? You could find the waiting very tiresome.'

'Tiresome is not a word I would have chosen,' he murmured, flame sparking in the depths of his eyes. 'The mere prospect of staying by your side for any length of time appears an immensely pleasurable one to me.' The husky, sexy undertone he used sent an echoing quiver whispering through her limbs.

'I wouldn't like,' she said raggedly, 'for you to be suffering from any illusions about our future relationship. I have the strong feeling that your expectations might be far different from mine, and I think you should know——'

He inclined his head briefly, his finger reaching out gently to stay the words on her lips. 'Do not make life so terribly complicated, *gatita*. It is the end of a long day, and you must learn to unwind.' Folding her hand within his own, he drew her towards the screen doors. 'We will go and sit on the terrace,' he asserted. 'You will enjoy the coffee and liqueurs Rosana has put out for us.'

The rooms of the house, she saw, led out on to a wide veranda, facing on to a paved courtyard, in the middle of which was a large, ornamental pool, a fountain, lit from behind, playing a soothing, spray-mist dance at its centre. On the flagstones, tubs of flowers were arranged, adding bright splashes of colour, their fragrance drifting on the warm air. Lanterns bathed the covered veranda with soft, golden light.

'You have a beautiful home,' she said quietly, her senses mellowing to the breathtaking perfection of everything around her. In a place like this, it would be all too easy to sink into the feather-bed luxury, to push into the background the problems of day-to-day living.

'I am pleased that it is to your liking,' he murmured, applying gentle pressure to her fingers as he tugged her towards a low, cushioned seat. 'Come and sit beside me. Will you take cream with your coffee? Mints?'

'Thank you.' She followed his bidding, a curious tremor running through her limbs as she slid down next to him, her concentration fixed on the long, hard muscularity of his body. As he leaned across to deal with the cups laid out on the small table in front of him, the warm, vital length of his thigh made breathtaking contact with her own and she was overwhelmingly conscious of his male, musky scent, the texture of his bronzed skin, the gleam of light on his crisp black hair.

Pausing, he turned suddenly to look at her, catching her absorbed appraisal. His well shaped mouth curved faintly, at once tantalisingly attractive, and his eyes glimmered, his glance moving over her in a purely sensual scrutiny that shook her to the core. A wave of heat washed through her, the tiny pulse in her throat beginning to throb with startled, erratic tension.

'My looking at you makes you nervous?' he murmured, seizing on that betraying flicker with unfailing perspicacity. 'Now why should that be? It is only natural, is it not, for me to look upon you with true appreciation?'

Her mind reeled as the heady intoxication of his sheer maleness curled around her senses. He liked to look at her, he'd said, and she was finding it impossible to wrench her gaze from him. He filled her vision; her sole instinct was to reach out and run her fingers over the compelling masculinity of that hard jaw, and then let them drift down to savour the feel of his strong, broad shoulders.

His gaze slid over the burnished gold of her hair, shifting to rest on the smooth curve of her cheek. 'You are irresistibly lovely—who could blame me for wanting to feast my eyes?' he queried in thickened tones. 'Your complexion is peaches and cream, your lips have all the luscious invitation of sun-ripened strawberries.' Unexpectedly, his arm slid around her, his other hand moving in a warm caress over her waist, drawing her towards him, compelling her with soft urgency into his coaxing embrace.

The touch of his lips was like the burn of hot silk on her waiting mouth. Her eyes closed as weakness invaded her body, the pleasure of that heated kiss filling every particle of her being. He explored the sweet secrets of her mouth with lips and tongue, a low, hungry growl of satisfaction rumbling in the back of his throat. Slowly, his hands shaped her, smoothing over the thin material of her dress and leaving behind a fiery trail of intense, exquisite sensation. As he moved closer, ever closer, she felt herself eased backwards into the enveloping softness of the plump cushions, and, shakily, she became aware of the warm glide of his thumb beneath her breast, the curve of his cupped palm nudging its heavy fullness. Her breath snagged in tingling, shocked perception. A fragment of elusive caution fluttered across her mind, and she tried to pull back, breaking away from that drugging kiss with shivery despair.

'You want me,' he muttered with deep sureness, taking in the dazed expression of her cornflower-blue eyes, the feverish glitter surfacing there. 'I feel it,' he murmured roughly. 'I feel your trembling response, yet you push me away. Why, *enamorada*? What is it that you fear? Do you think I would harm you?' He smiled suddenly, and her heart lurched, her will-power shattered by the devastating appeal of that firm mouth, his features changing in a way that tugged dangerously at her senses. Slowly, his hands began to move on her arms, his thumbs making warm, lazy circles. 'Surely you do not believe that.'

Awareness was a tangible thing, arcing between them like the crackle of electricity. There was heady enticement in the gleaming depths of his eyes, enough heat emanating from him to start a blaze. In growing agitation, she tried to resist his sensual lure, unhappily conscious all the while of the shameful melting of her limbs, of the treacherous movement of her body towards him, of her aching need to be kissed again, and feel his hands shaping her softness.

A sound coming from somewhere behind them broke the spell. She moved back in the same instant, her nerves jangled by the sudden intrusion, only then realising how close she had come to surrendering to the piercing demands of her body. She had never before experienced such a burning desire to touch and be touched. Why had it happened now, with this man? It would be her undoing, to allow herself to be bewitched by his dark sorcery. To him, it was a means to an end, a pleasurable interlude, a ruse to undermine her self-control and win her to his side.

Rosana, clearing away the dishes in the dining-room beyond, had been her saviour. She breathed a thankful sigh and glanced at Alejo, marking the narrowing of his eyes, the tense closure of his expression.

'My housekeeper is intent on her duties,' he muttered through gritted teeth. 'I shall send her away.'

'No.' Deanna stopped him with the sharply uttered syllable, shivering slightly as he turned to her with a darkly questioning glance. 'Please don't do that,' she said. 'I... it's late, and I think I should like to go to my room now.' Her head was clearing rapidly, and the knowledge of the true extent of her foolishness was beginning to sweep over her. He wanted her softened and malleable, willing to give him every last scrap of information she had, yet when he was done with her she would be cast aside, like so much flotsam washed up on a deserted beach.

He had the power to inflict lasting wounds, and she was not ready to submit herself once more to that slow torture. She had been through it all with Richard, who had deceived her with another woman, playing fast and loose with her emotions. Men thought about sex in a different way from women. To them it was a need, a matter of brief urgency, without regard to deep, inner feelings.

'A few moments ago,' he said tersely, 'you were returning my kisses with scant reserve. What has brought about this change in you, this so sudden coolness? Have you just now remembered your absent lover, the man who leaves you behind without a backward glance? You waste your time in thoughts of him. He can offer you nothing. Better that you tell me where I might find him, so that you can face him with his worthlessness.'

'That's what all this has been about, isn't it?' she said with harsh accusation. 'What you can't get with outright demand, you think you can sneak from me with soft seduction.' Her mouth tightened in pained rejection. 'It won't work, not ever. I'm not to be used in that way. And I've not forgotten Luis—how could I? And he would never have behaved in the way that you do. He's a man of honour,' she defended with fierce conviction, watching with unhappy frustration the way his lips curled in quick contempt. He discounted her beliefs without a second thought, and there was no way she could see to persuade him otherwise. He had made up his mind, too, that Luis was her lover, and perhaps that was no bad thing, in the end, if it might dissuade him in some small way from pursuing her.

'He does not deserve your rush to defend him.' His face was tight, his hands clenching. 'How can you continue to respect a man who turns and runs instead of facing up to the consequences of his actions?'

'He's done nothing wrong. Can you blame the fox for running from those who would tear him to pieces? You are his persecutor, you would see him rot in gaol for something he has not done, and you would throw away the key, forget that he ever existed.' She jumped up from the low couch, anguish twisting her features. 'What was I thinking of? How could I have let you touch me, make love to me? When I think of what I've done——'

Coming to his feet alongside her, he caught her when she would have turned away, dragging her to him so that she was held fast against his rugged male strength, and she was made vibrantly aware of rigidly controlled muscle and sinew.

'You think you have betrayed him?' he said raspingly. 'It is true. A few more moments, and you would have been sighing in my arms. You cannot deny it, and I take pleasure in the knowledge that you would have been mine.'

'No,' she denied shakily. 'Never—a few kisses—what is that? I shall wipe the memory of them from my mouth, from my mind. You have no hold over me. My loyalty is with Luis. It will always be with him. You condemn him, but you're far, far worse.

You used me to get at him; you wanted to steal your way into my confidence so that I would breach his trust, and I'm telling you, you'll never succeed in that, because I know nothing, do you hear? He wanted to protect me and he has told me nothing.'

His fingers tightened on her arms. 'Again this plea of the *ingénue*—do you imagine that I am to be so easily fooled? Think again, my beautiful deceiver.' Scorn etched his mouth, his dark gaze piercing her like the touch of steel. 'You have hindered me, sent me off on some wild-goose chase, and you have tried to elude me every step of the way. You are not to be trusted.' His grip on her loosened, his hands sliding along her arms in a sensual caress that sent the blood racing through her veins like quicksilver on a hot summer's day. 'There is but one thing in your favour——' His fingers paused, then began a slow, exploratory trail along the sensitive inner skin of her forearm. 'I am prepared to overlook your behaviour, *enamorada*. I am a very wealthy man, and you will find that I can be more than generous, should the occasion arise. Tell me what I want to know, and the world is yours.'

Deanna bit back a long, shuddery breath. She had been right to despise him, to delve deeper into his true intentions. He did not want her for herself. He wanted only the satisfaction of reaching the goal he had set, and he had no qualms about who was hurt on the way. Poor Luis, to be pursued by such a man.

She drew on her reserves of pride and self-control. 'I am not to be bought,' she said with icy calm. 'You may have wealth and influence, but they hold no sway whatever with me.'

His granite-chiselled features were sculpted in cynicism. 'That is a statement yet to be tested,' he said coolly. 'But for the moment, since you are obviously still suffering the wearisome effects of your manoeuvrings over the last few days, I shall bid you goodnight. Tomorrow, I have no doubt, you will begin to appreciate the inherent folly of setting yourself against me.'

'Tomorrow,' she answered with sharp-edged vehemence, 'I shall leave here, and put this whole sorry episode behind me. If it were at all within my power, I would leave now, and not impose on you any longer, but as that is clearly out of the question I shall thank you for your hospitality and be out of here at the earliest possible moment.'

She left him, and went up to her room, making her preparations for bed with frowning preoccupation. He had implied that this was not yet over; there had been a subtle threat underlying his words. But what could he do, in reality? What options were open to him? A shiver ran through her. She did not dare think what plans were brewing in his dark, devious mind. Only one thing she knew for certain. She had to get away from here, away from him, at the first opportunity.

Her chance came, sooner than she had expected. Rosana served her with breakfast in the dining-room, bringing in hot, crispy rolls, with a selection of honey and preserves. Alejo was nowhere to be seen.

'He breakfasted earlier,' Rosana told her in answer to her query. 'He had urgent matters to attend to on the plantation, and he regrets that he is unable to join you this morning. A car and driver will be placed at your disposal, whenever you are ready to leave.' The older woman smiled, busying herself with setting out dishes on the table. 'But you eat first,' she instructed. 'I will bring for you whatever you want. Eggs? Ham? You tell me.'

'Nothing, thank you.' Deanna shook her head. 'This is just perfect.'

Rosana made a clucking noise like a mother hen disturbed by a recalcitrant chick. Her greying hair was wound up neatly in a silky knot at the back of her head, but she fussed with it, as though she would have order in that at least. Pouring coffee, then juice, she checked the table once more, assuring herself that all was well, before she went back to the kitchen.

Deanna ate slowly, deeply thoughtful. Her relief at being given the freedom to leave as she pleased, without hindrance, was tinged with suspicion. Had he finally come to believe her? After a good night's sleep, had he decided that enough time had been wasted in futile questioning and that there was no more to be done? He was not, after all, a man of leisure; there was this huge plantation to be run, a workforce to be organised, and a mere girl surely did not merit more than a moment's attention.

Within half an hour, she was ready to go. To delay might have meant running into Alejo once more, and that was something she definitely did not want to do. Out of sight, out of mind. It had never struck her as a particularly meaningful saying before, but now it seemed more than apt, given the circumstances. Now that he was back from the States, his work would occupy him fully, and he would scarcely be bothered with a young woman forty or so miles distant. The sooner she was out of here the better.

The driver loaded up the car with her packages and overnight case, and with a final wave to Rosana Deanna slid into the passenger seat and settled back for the journey to Lakuno.

CHAPTER FIVE

'SO YOU'RE back safely,' Carmela said as Deanna walked into the office a couple of hours later. 'I was a little worried when I felt the earth tremors. Did you feel them? I know they weren't very strong, but I wasn't sure where they were coming from.'

'I felt the earth shaking a little as I came through the hills,' Deanna answered, pushing boxes of supplies on to the table, 'but I think the main centre must be higher up, in the west. Like you, I wasn't sure whether it was anything to be concerned about, but the driver didn't appear bothered by them, and they're fairly usual around here, I think.'

Carmela seemed reassured by that. 'You were stuck in Cacheni, weren't you? Someone from a garage delivered your truck about half an hour ago—he said you'd made other arrangements. From the looks of things you managed to find transport, anyway.'

Deanna did not feel up to sharing her experiences just yet. Instead, she looked smilingly at her friend, and said, 'I did, and I'm glad to be back. I tried to ring you yesterday, but you must have been away.'

'I was supposed to be meeting José,' Carmela said, a rueful grimace settling on her pretty, oval-shaped face. 'Why do I bother with that man, do you know? I am sure I don't. It is always promises,

promises, sweetness and light, and then I am left on my own while he goes off on yet another photographic mission somewhere across the world. I hardly ever see him. I am sure he has someone else.' She sighed, hazel eyes troubled and uncertain. 'Men. Why do we allow them to turn our lives upside-down?'

Deanna shared with her that familiar chord of feeling, but to have voiced it would not have helped Carmela. 'Perhaps you're mistaken,' she murmured. 'He comes back readily enough to you each time, doesn't he?'

Carmela thought about it. 'I suppose you could be right,' she admitted doubtfully. 'But I must not spend time going over my problems while the work is piling up here.' Her glance skimmed over the packages with approval. 'I am glad to see that you brought the antibiotics and the distilled water. We were getting desperately short.'

Deanna nodded. 'I'll make up the schedules for the drivers, then we can get them distributed tomorrow.'

Going over to her desk in a corner of the room, she sat down and pulled a file from her drawer. She worked for several hours, with only an occasional break for coffee, checking lists and quantities, re-checking her work whenever images of a smiling, dark-eyed predator loomed in the recesses of her mind. A headache throbbed faintly at her temples, a result of the tension that had held her fast all morning. Why did Alejo de Rocas continually break into her thoughts? He had no business there. It was this heat that was disturbing her, wasn't it, this slow build-up of hot, humid air, steadily mounting to a crescendo that would only be alleviated by the threatening rain? She was glad of her sleeveless white blouse, and her cool linen skirt.

Hearing a noise from the front of the building, Carmela moved to the window and looked out, giving a little cry of delight. 'He is back,' she said joyfully. 'Now I am all cheered up. No more doldrums, you will see.' She ran to the door, and Deanna heard gravel scattering in all directions as a vehicle pulled to a stop outside. She smiled, and stretched, happy for her friend, though the thought crossed her mind that it wasn't at all usual for José to drive with such vigour on to their frontage. His step sounded unusually brisk, too.

'Why did you not tell me you were coming over?' Carmela was saying as she came through the door, her black hair rippling in glossy waves as she tilted her head to look at the man who followed her. Deanna's attention swung in their direction, and her smile died a sudden death, her stomach muscles tightening in an involuntary spasm.

'You have hardly contacted me for weeks,' Carmela pouted. 'The occasional phone call, what use is that? I ask you. None at all.'

'It keeps me informed, and it keeps you on your toes,' Alejo de Rocas said with a gleam in his eye that belied his severe tone.

Carmela turned and stood in front of him. 'I have missed you,' she said, running her manicured fingers up over his pale blue shirt.

Dressed in cream trousers, his matching jacket worn loose, he looked cool and commanding, and in this small office somehow taller, more overpowering, if that was possible. Deanna's mouth was dry, her eyes growing large and round with stunned disbelief. What was he doing here? So soon, too. She had hoped... And what was this between him and Carmela? She was sliding her hands over his chest with an annoying familiarity that made Deanna tighten her knuckles whitely as she pretended to be engrossed in her paperwork. Alejo was enjoying it, too; there was a widening grin on his face, he was actually laughing down at Carmela. Laughing. Deanna's throat closed up.

'So you have missed me, have you?' he enquired of Carmela in an amused tone. 'And what of José, your boyfriend? Has he not been keeping you occupied and out of mischief?'

Carmela lifted an expressive shoulder. 'He flew to London yesterday,' she told him, her eyes darkly smouldering, half slitted. 'With that pale-faced journalist. I think he is not faithful to me, you know. I think it is finished with him and me.'

Alejo's mouth kept its curve as his arms wound around her, hugging her to him. '*Está bien*. His loss is my gain, then.'

Deanna looked away, searching through the file on her desk for a list of supplies whose relevance to anything had for the moment escaped her. She was not jealous, she told herself. Of course she was not jealous. So what, if he wanted to play flirtatious games with her colleague? Let him. Let them both enjoy their touching reunion; it didn't matter a jot to her that they couldn't keep their hands off each other, did it? Her fingers closed with breaking force on her pencil, her shoulders were rigid, her back stiff and unyielding as the arguments raged inside her.

'Has no one told you,' Alejo asked drily, coming to stand in front of her desk, and looking at her with cool, dark eyes, 'that it is not good to glare in such a fashion? It might give the impression that you are not pleased to see me. That will not do at all, will it? Especially after I have gone to so much trouble to get here.'

'And so quickly,' she muttered in reply. 'But why concern yourself with my reactions? You've made Carmela's day absolutely perfect for her; isn't that enough for you?'

His mouth made a cold twist. 'You will soon become used to my presence,' he assured her. 'You will find that I shall be very much in evidence over the next few weeks.'

Deanna's frown deepened, and Carmela, looking slightly puzzled, but otherwise unaffected by their interchange, said, 'I had no idea that you two had met already, but perhaps I should explain, Deanna, that the Rocas family have had a financial interest in the Centre for many years. It is not something that is widely known, because Alejo has always preferred his name to be kept in the background.'

Deanna felt the colour draining from her face. 'I see.' She ought to have known. It ought to have been clear to her all along that she had no chance of escaping him, that he was going to turn up and haunt her life like some oppressive black cloud forever looming over her. He was even more powerful than she had imagined, it appeared, but exactly what kind of threat did he pose for her? Could her job be at stake if she continued to stand against him? A shiver of unease whispered along her spine, chilling her to the bone. He had her in the palm of his hand, and all he had to do was close his fingers and crush her.

Outside, a truck pulled up with a heavy grinding of brakes, and Carmela said, 'I will go and deal with that. It is probably the gauze and suchlike that we ordered.'

Deanna stared bleakly ahead, conscious only of Alejo's mocking smile.

He bent slowly towards her, the pads of his fingers spread out on the table, pressing down, strong and firmly immovable. 'You will find,' he murmured, his voice low and subtly infused with disturbing overtones of menace, 'that wealth and influence do, despite your declarations to the contrary, have their place in the grand scheme of things, after all. From now on, you may expect that I shall be here, on the scene, so to speak, to monitor your movements and counter any subterfuge that you and your cheating lover might be planning between you.'

'Won't that be rather difficult,' she queried, her voice not nearly as steady as she would have liked, 'given that you live several miles from here? Much as you may have this fiendish desire to shadow me, I'm afraid you might find yourself encountering a few problems along the way.'

'Do not let those considerations occupy your mind,' he advised her, straightening. 'I have already made arrangements to stay in the apartment that was built next to the new wing. It will give me an opportunity to study at closer range the workings of the Centre, among other things.' His glittering gaze left her in no doubt as to what those other things might be.

'I should have thought,' she commented tersely, 'that you could use your influence in other, more effective ways.'

'An admirable suggestion,' he agreed. 'It has already been acted upon, of course. The *policía* were informed some time ago, and the appropriate wheels were set in motion to find San Martin.' She drew in a sharp breath, which brought his black brows winging together. 'You are alarmed by this? Put aside your concern. The authorities know well how to deal with villains—which reminds me——' He paused, lifting a hand to reach into a pocket inside his jacket. 'This was returned to me this morning.' He tossed her purse on to the table. 'You are fortunate that our police are so efficient, are you not?'

Her breathing had still not settled to an even pace. Fear for Luis left her stricken. 'Thank you,' she managed. 'I hadn't expected to see it again. It was very thoughtful of you to go to so much trouble on my behalf.' She swallowed, then said huskily, 'Did you really have to bring in the police to help in your search for Luis?'

'It was necessary,' he confirmed briskly, then allowed himself a brief smile which set her nerves leaping all over again. 'You, however, are a different matter altogether, *enamorada*. Keeping tabs on you is a task I reserve purely for myself.' His glance shimmered over her, and she wondered despairingly why it was that such a man could throw her senses into hopeless, chaotic turmoil with a mere look, or simple gesture. Her whole body was on edge, vibrating with locked-in tension like a coiled spring.

'There is no future in following me,' she told him abstractedly. 'I heard you were ruthless, and now I can see that it's true. This whole thing is like a mission of venegeance; you persist as though Luis has done something dreadfully wrong, and that can't be so. There was no need to call in the police.'

He looked at her with cold astonishment. 'You suggested it yourself, did you not? You believed I could bring my influence to bear in other ways.'

'I didn't think for one minute that you would do it. I thought perhaps it would make you realise how absurd this is; that you were placing too much importance on a minor incident.'

Stark silence fell on the room for a few moments. Then he spoke, his voice grating harshly with the low rumble of anger. 'You call theft *minor*? I cannot believe that I heard you say that. You did not mind the loss of your purse? Perhaps I should have thrown it away, disposed of it in the river, if it is of so little importance to you?'

'No, no, you misunderstand me,' she said in agitation. 'Luis——'

'Luis is a thief,' he cut in brutally. 'He was entrusted with the task of cataloguing my collection of Peruvian artefacts, and he repaid that trust by removing two pots.' The hard-boned contours of his face were etched in savage contempt. 'They are reputedly worth many thousands of pounds. I do not call that a matter of *minor* importance.'

Deanna stared at him, disbelief thundering across her mind, shock making her blood pound in heavy, discordant waves, the roar of it echoing in her ears. 'He wouldn't have done that,' she said in ragged earnestness. 'He couldn't have done anything like that.' She searched his face for signs of a lie, anything, to give her reason to discount what he had said. 'You were in the States,' she said. 'How could you have known that this had happened?'

'Do you seriously imagine that because I am away I have no idea what is the state of my affairs?' His tone strafed her with wrathful disparagement. 'I am kept very well informed of what goes on, both in my business and my household. Your dear Luis thought he could cheat me, by replacing my treasures with fakes, but he was soon to be sadly disillusioned on that score.'

'You're wrong,' Deanna said shakily. 'There must be some other explanation for what has happened. You've known Luis for only a few short months, whereas I've known him since I was in my teens, and I would trust him with my life. My parents would vouch for him, I'm certain. The evidence might point to his guilt, but you can't know that for certain, can you? It looks that way, I grant you, but things aren't always what they seem.'

'It would seem that he has well and truly filled your head with sweet images of him, so much that you are dazzled by the light of his halo.'

'No,' she said. 'That isn't the way it is. Why would he put his career at risk by doing such a thing?'

'Perhaps he thought it a risk worth taking. He must have believed that the money he gained from the sale of the stolen goods would set him up for life—and he would not have been far wrong in that assumption. Forgery, and smuggling, are big business.'

Deanna shook her head. 'You're not talking about the man I know.'

His eyes darkened. 'You require proof?' Once more, he reached inside his jacket pocket and drew out a small, folded piece of paper. 'It is a photocopy,' he said, pushing it towards her, 'but you will see that it shows how he attempted to obtain the services of a respected craftsman. In doing that, he made a grave error of judgement, because the craftsman came to me.'

Deanna stared at the paper, the words blurring in front of her eyes. 'In respect of services to be fulfilled... Items to be collected...'

'No, no, I don't believe it,' she whispered.

'In the face of this evidence, it is clear that he decided to flee.'

Still she would not accept what he was saying. 'Why would he have put anything in writing? This, in itself, could be a forgery. Your respected craftsman could be a rogue.' Had Luis stumbled on to something—was that why he was wary of being followed?

'Then where is your Luis now?' he persisted with ruthless determination. 'And where is my property?'

She moistened her dry lips. 'He's innocent. I feel it—instinctively, deep inside, I feel it.'

He brushed aside her convictions with sardonic disregard. 'I place no faith in this instinct of yours. Passion, intoxication of the senses, these are the feelings more likely to influence your emotions where this man is concerned. I care nothing for your tender expressions of loyalty.' His gaze swept grimly over her. 'More likely you are working in this together. That is why your knowledge of Peruvian culture extends so far. You are a team, you collude, one with the other.'

'You're insulting,' she flung at him. 'You may have been wronged, but I'm not going to stand in as your whipping-boy. And don't think that I shall meekly allow you to interfere with my life. I'm a free person, I shall do as I please, go where I please, and if you try to turn that to your advantage I shall fight you, every step of the way.'

'And I shall look forward to the battle, *gatita*,' he acknowledged with unrelenting vigour. 'Be warned, there are limits to this freedom, and I am here to exercise them.'

Carmela came back into the office and looked from one to the other in frank dismay. 'From the sound of raised voices,' she said, 'it's just as well that I am here to stop you from coming to blows. Heavens, I only left you together for a few moments. It must be the heat that is fraying tempers this afternoon. No matter, the rain has started. That will cool things down a little.'

The ringing of the phone sounded another jarring note, and Deanna picked up the receiver, biting back a startled exclamation as she heard Luis's voice on the end of the line. 'One moment, please,' she said briskly, as though she was addressing someone in a purely business fashion. Holding the receiver against her blouse, she said to Carmela, 'Why don't you take our visitor to see the new wing? He tells me that he's interested in the accommodation there.'

'I don't doubt it, since he paid for it,' Carmela said laughingly. 'It is a very good idea, Alejo. It might put you in a better frame of mind. My friend seems to have a rather odd effect on you.'

Alejo's eyes narrowed, his gaze sharpening on the telephone receiver which Deanna cradled to her. She smiled sweetly, waiting for them to leave, and he said thoughtfully, 'It is true. She is a particularly provoking individual.'

Deanna waited until they had left the office before returning to her phone call. 'Luis,' she said in a voice little above a whisper, 'what is happening? Where are you?'

'Deanna,' he said urgently, 'I need to ask your help. I must have some antibiotics—I have a slight wound which is, I think, beginning to be infected——'

'A wound?' she cut in sharply, 'But how bad is it? How did it——?'

'Listen...please listen, do not talk, I do not have long enough. It is nothing to worry about,' he told her. 'I am going to the lodge that was once used by biologists—you will remember it, Deanna? I showed it to you once. It is at the very edge of the jungle—you should be able to get there by road from the Centre. Will you do that for me?'

'Yes, of course I will, but you must tell me more. I've heard all kinds of things—talk of theft and forgery——'

'I can't talk now. It is a long story, but I will tell you everything when we meet. I am innocent, believe me. Try not to worry, and whatever you do, do not tell anyone where I am.'

'But Señor de Rocas——' she began, only to be swiftly silenced by his hurried interruption.

'He must not know where I am. If he becomes any more deeply involved, he will be stirring up a hornets' nest. This thing is far bigger than I had imagined. I have uncovered too much already. I do not know whom I can trust, even in his household, and should word get out about my hiding place it could mean my life. Be silent for me, Deanna. Will you do this for me? Will you try?'

Shocked, she answered with a shake in her voice, 'I'll do my best. Luis——'

'Thank you. There is one thing more—did you receive the parcel I sent?'

Frowning, she said hesitantly, 'Parcel? No, there hasn't been any——'

'No matter,' he said. 'It should arrive any day now. Take care of it for me, will you, until I return? Goodbye, Deanna.'

'Luis, what——?' It was a wasted plea. He had cut the call.

Her mind was churning with questions that would not be answered. What had happened to Luis? Why was his life in danger? How had he been wounded? A shiver tore through her. These men who were after him—did they carry weapons... guns?

She stared at the telephone for some time, unseeing, her thoughts running over the events of the last few days again and again. Outside, the rain was falling in a steady downpour; she could hear the hiss of it, the heavy rattle against the windowpanes. The afternoon was already wearing away, and the journey to the lodge would take several hours. Would she make it before nightfall? It didn't seem likely, but Luis was asking for help, and she at least had to try.

'It appears that the call has done nothing to lighten your mood,' Alejo remarked as he walked back into the room with Carmela in tow. 'Have you been presented with a problem of some sort?' The lambent glow of speculation was reflected in his deep brown eyes. 'I am here to help with such matters. Tell me what has occurred.'

'There's no need,' she muttered, taxing her brain to find a way out of the situation. 'It's just a small hiccup, something I can deal with quite adequately by myself.' He was suspicious, she knew, and he was a man of his word, she had learned that lesson well enough—every move she made would be under the microscope of his scrutiny from now on. Somehow she had to give him the slip. 'I think some coffee is called for, don't you?' she said, smiling lightly and walking over to the filter machine as though she didn't have a care in the world. 'Did you find the apartment to your liking?'

He was not fooled by her change of subject, she sensed that from the slight hardening of his mouth, but to her relief he did not pursue the matter. 'Everything is just as I would have expected,' he answered, accepting the cup she handed to him.

'That's good. Do you have your luggage with you, or are you travelling back to the plantation to pick it up?' She sipped delicately at her own drink.

His mouth curved faintly. 'Rest assured, Deanna, it is all taken care of. I have everything I need right here.'

She might have known it. She kept her smile firmly in place. 'You are so organised,' she said. 'Will you need any help installing your belongings? I'm rather busy at the moment, but I'm sure Carmela would love to give you a hand if you need one.' She raised her brows questioningly towards the other girl, and Carmela nodded with bright enthusiasm.

'I was going to suggest it,' she said. 'In fact, though, before we do that, I wanted to show you the new addition to our little community.'

Alejo studied her. 'What addition is this?'

Carmela was happy to oblige with details. 'An alpaca wandered down from the hills a few weeks ago,' she explained, 'and we put her in the barn. She's such a tiny thing, and she looked so bedraggled and forlorn, we couldn't bear to set her loose straight away.'

'A few weeks?' Alejo queried. 'Should she not have been sent back to the hills before this, to her own kind?'

Carmela laughed. 'Don't think we haven't tried. It is all Deanna's fault, you know.' She grinned at the quick colour that came into Deanna's face, and went on, 'It was the first few nights that caused the problem, you see. The poor little thing was so miserable that Deanna stayed up with her much of the time, and now she follows her everywhere. Every time we try to send her back to the hills, she comes back to us—well, to Deanna. We call her Junket because she drinks and drinks, and then she does a kind of shaky dance all around the compound. We are sure she is making cheese.' She put down her coffee cup. 'Come and see.'

Alejo's lips curved. 'How can I miss this? Lead the way.'

Once they had gone, Deanna hurried into action. It was not a chance she would get again, and she could only rely on a few minutes' grace at the most. Scribbling a brief message for Carmela, to tell her that she had set out to make a local delivery, she made up a small package of things she thought she would need, pulled on a light cotton jacket, then rushed outside to the pick-up truck.

Rain soaked through the thin material as she ran, but she ignored it, climbing quickly into the cab and turning the key in the ignition. It started first time and she sent up a heartfelt prayer of thanks that the mechanics had managed to sort out the problem. Five minutes later, she was on the road, heading towards the lodge.

Gradually, she realised that she might, in some small way, begin to relax. Loosening her tortured grip on the wheel a fraction, she allowed herself a grim smile. He was not following. How could he, anyway, when she had a head start, and he did not know where she was going? She peered out through the windscreen, the wipers working overtime to sweep away the constant stream of water. It did not make for good driving conditions, this rain. The dusty roads turned to mud in the torrent, slippery and treacherous. She could feel the slight skid of the wheels as she took the bends. Perhaps she should slow down a little. Breaking her neck was not going to help Luis in any way at all, was it?

It was just as well that she did slow down, because the mud slide waiting around the corner could have been the finish of her. Instead, the wheels ploughed into it, skated in a wildly rippling arc, and flung the pick-up with bone-shaking ferocity to a standstill against the sloping hillside. She jerked forward, then back, her head slamming against the solid head-rest.

Time passed. How much, she did not know, but after a while she shifted slowly and stared, without focusing, at the windscreen. Even doing that seemed like too much of an effort. Her eyelids were heavy; lead weights were forcing them down. There was a crunching sound from outside the vehicle, the small truck swayed with some wrenching movement, and she closed her eyes wearily.

'*Infierno!*' It was a deep, growling sound that sent dark imaginings quivering along her nervous system. The black panther had come to get her, her attempt to escape had been futile from the beginning, it had come to nothing, and now the sleek, dark predator was prowling around her, its golden eyes searing her with lethal intensity. '*Que pasa?* Deanna?' A stream of incomprehensible Spanish followed, and from some vague point in its midst she slowly opened her eyes again.

Not a panther. A jagged line furrowed her brow. Raven-black hair, granite-cut features, eyes that burned. '*Di...diablo*,' she muttered. The devil had come to get her. She was lost, it was done; she would be devoured by the leaping, shuddering flames.

'Deanna, are you hurt? Speak to me.' Alejo's gravelly voice, thickly accented, at last impinged itself on her consciousness, and she shifted her head slightly, looking up at him in dazed bewilderment, wondering why he was there, why his arms were folded around her, what her head was doing nestled up against that broad chest. It did not make sense; it seemed wrong, somehow, to be wrapped up in such a way, for everything to be so still, just the strong, heavy beat of his heart thudding steadily beneath her temple. Restful, though, it was so restful, and the temptation simply to lie there and do nothing was infinitely sweet.

'Deanna,' he said again, more abrasively this time, and she frowned.

'Mustn't shout,' she mumbled into his shirtfront, her mouth pressured by the warm, muscled hardness of his chest.

'Are you in pain? Tell me.'

She sensed the grit in his voice, the tough, demanding urgency of his questions. Why wouldn't he leave her alone, let her drift back into that welcoming black void? 'S'aright,' she muttered incoherently. 'S'all right. Head. Headache.'

Cool fingers slid through the silky tangle of her hair, explored her skull with gentle expertise, and she breathed deeply, relaxing under the careful ministration of those large, competent hands. When he stopped touching her and moved away, it was a feeling of utter loss. After a few moments, though, the comfort returned, as he produced a damp cloth, and pressed it to the back of her head.

She sighed deeply. 'That feels much better,' she said.

'You will be well enough soon.' His tone was crisp, curt almost, and she blinked, opening her eyes wide, looking at him afresh.

'Thank you,' she murmured. 'Thank you for helping me.' She frowned again as memory stirred. 'I seem to be saying that a lot just lately, don't I? Why are you here, anyway? You shouldn't be here, should you?'

'It is just as well for you that I was able to follow your tracks,' he said roughly, his mouth making a hard, slashing line. 'That was an incredibly foolish thing you did, taking off like that. *Idiota*. This is no country road, back in England. This is the Amazon. It is *peligroso*; there is much danger.'

'I know,' she said carefully, taking her time over the words, 'about the Amazon. There is no need for you to growl at me.'

'If I were to follow my true instinct,' he said with marked emphasis, 'you would have far more to complain about. You have behaved with breathtaking lack of thought. Even a child would have more sense. To drive off without leaving any record of where you could be found was the height of stupidity. It is no wonder I lose patience with you.' His gaze raked her with the cutting precision of a laser. 'Where did you think you were going, anyway?'

'I was...' She thought about it, her mind busily trying to sift through the cluttered mass of intentions to find the right one. 'I had to...' Pausing with bleak uncertainty, she let her glance drift around the cab for inspiration until she caught sight of the package wedged into the open glove compartment. Memory returned in full measure, the extent of what she had been about to give away hitting her with full force. She clamped her lips together. Of all the devious, underhand... he had known exactly what he was doing, hadn't he, probing like that when she wasn't fully herself?

'You had to...what?' he echoed, a glint sparking to life in those dangerous, altogether too perceptive eyes.

'Something,' she said vaguely. 'The bang on my head must have made things a little foggy.'

'I have no doubt,' he said drily, 'that the fog will clear soon enough, when it suits you.'

She raised a finely sculpted brow. 'I have no idea what you mean. Is it important that you know the detail of my plans? It was just a local delivery; I think that was what I put in my note to Carmela.

Why don't you go back to the Centre and tell her that I'm quite well? I'll just sit here a moment and get myself together, and then I'll follow.'

'That is not a good idea,' he stated firmly, dismissing the suggestion with all the hauteur inherent in his ancestry. '*No me gusta*. I do not like it. At all. So, we will make it the other way around. I will get your truck back on the road, and then *I* will follow *you* back to the Centre.'

The set of his mouth brooked no argument, and she could see that she had no choice but to submit reluctantly. It was late, anyway, she told herself dismally. There was no way she could reach Luis now, before nightfall. All she could do was to try again, tomorrow.

CHAPTER SIX

CARMELA appeared at the door to the Centre as Deanna achingly stepped down from the truck. 'This parcel came for you soon after you left,' she said, holding up a large box. 'It was sent by special delivery.' Hazel eyes studied her carefully. 'Are you all right, Deanna? You are definitely looking a bit peaky.'

'She has a headache,' Alejo informed her brusquely. 'A rather major one, I should imagine.' His tone, with a subtle spicing of innuendo meant for Deanna alone, implied that it was not only the result of the bang she had received.

Deanna sent him a fraught stare. He knew very well that he had blocked her attempt to go to Luis by insisting that he follow her back here, and it was patently obvious that she would now have to find another way of slipping out to meet him. He had set himself in the role of her tormentor, and he must be getting a real kick out of seeing her in this predicament.

If only he would believe what she had been trying to tell him—that Luis was not capable of doing anything dishonest...if he could in some small way accept the possibility that her feelings were not totally irrational... Disconsolately, she pushed away the futile train of thought. The slant of his hard mouth had an edge of cruelty that gave her no hope that he might relent in the slightest part.

Relieving Carmela of the parcel, she said, 'Thanks. I'm fine, really. I think I'll go along to my flat, though, and freshen up.' She cast a glance over the darkening skyline and asked, 'Are you going home now? We've finished everything for today, haven't we?'

'I'm on my way, just as soon as I've locked up.'

'I shall do it,' Alejo said, and Deanna watched in mute annoyance as he walked through to the office and removed the keys from the small cabinet fixed to the wall. He had only been here five minutes and he was taking over. 'You go, Carmela,' he ordered. 'There is no need for you to wait, but take care, the roads are treacherous.'

'I shall, and anyway, it isn't far to my cottage,' Carmela told him. 'Thanks. I shall see you both in the morning.'

Deanna returned the other girl's wave, apprehension building up in her as she recognised that once Carmela had gone she would be quite alone in this place with Alejo. She was not up to any more confrontations with him right now; her emotions were too churned up inside her for her to be able to deal with him in any logical manner. She needed her wits about her.

When she had been hurt, he had been compassionate, caring, but she sensed that he would have done the same for any person in such a situation. It didn't mean that he felt anything for her, did it? His cool, curt manner since then had successfully annihilated any such possibility. It would be the ultimate folly secretly to treasure those moments when she had been gathered up in his arms, held fast in that refuge of strength and security. It could only lead to heartache, that was for sure.

'I could finish locking up,' she said to him. 'I'm sure you must want to get settled into your apartment.'

'Attend to your own needs,' he returned briskly. 'You look like a wraith, and I will not have your early demise on my conscience.'

His cold dismissal was what she might have expected, but the sting was no less for that. Turning, she hurried through to her own flat which adjoined the main block of the Centre. Shedding her jacket in her small hallway, she looked at the parcel, turning it over in her hands. This must be the one that Luis had spoken about, but it would have to wait until later. Right now, what she needed was to soak in the bath, and ease some of her stiffness away. The bump in the pick-up had shaken her more than she had realised at the time, and the after effects were just beginning to make themselves known.

The heat of the water was soothing, and she added a generous helping of perfumed bath oil, which gave her even more of an excuse to linger. Eventually, though, she had to concede that all good things must come to an end some time, and pangs of hunger were making her aware that she had not yet eaten. Slipping a silk embroidered robe over her underwear, she fastened the belt and wandered through to the kitchen to make herself a light salad.

What was it that Luis wanted her to keep for him? she wondered, finishing off the last of her meal and returning to the sitting-room. The package was certainly well wrapped up. It took more than a few minutes and the aid of a sharp-edged knife to slice through the thick covering, but when she finally laid bare the contents it was not relief that she felt, but complete and utter dismay.

The warm, rich colour of gold glimmered up at her from its bed of tissue, and with trembling fingers she lifted out the first of two jewel-encrusted pots, staring at it in disbelief. A gasp of incredulity hovered on her lips as her bewildered gaze took in the dazzling green fire, glinting sparks from the myriad facets of finely cut emeralds, and the glowing splendour of rubies which were embedded in the gold.

When the knocking on the door began, she jumped almost guiltily at the intrusion, and thrust the vessel quickly back into its box with its partner, pushing everything on to a low table at the side of the couch. Perhaps she shouldn't have opened it.

'Take care of it for me,' Luis had said. What on earth was going on? she wondered helplessly. Why had Luis sent the pots to her? Were they fakes? An inner feeling of dread told her that they were not. She struggled with the problem for several minutes, but it was hard to fathom the reasoning behind his actions. When she saw him again, surely it would all be explained?

The banging on the door increased in volume, sharp, peremptory, a staccato command that jangled her nerves and had her rushing to answer it.

'I was beginning to think,' Alejo said drily, 'that your accident this afternoon had left you more seriously affected than I had supposed. I was getting ready to break down the door.'

Deanna stared at him in frantic confusion. What was she to do? His priceless *objets d'art*—for she was almost certain that they were his—were sitting in her room, open for all to see, and how on earth could she explain away their presence? Ought she to tell him what had happened? But if she did that it would ensure that Luis sank further into the mire, and she couldn't be responsible for that, could she? Only one other alternative came to mind: she could see to it that he returned them personally to Alejo— that would be the best thing to do, wouldn't it?

Alejo looked at her closely. 'You are still pale,' he stated. 'Are you not well? You are feeling sick, perhaps?'

She tried to shift her gaze from his long, lithe frame. Even without this added problem of Luis, he was altogether too much, filling her doorway, his vital masculinity an inherent threat to her peace of mind. Huskily, she said, 'Thank you for your concern, but I'm perfectly well. There's no need for you to trouble yourself over me.' Pushing lightly on the door, she hoped he would take the hint and go. She had to be alone, to think, to decide what she was to do.

He was impervious to subtle suggestion, she discovered a moment later, as he remained solidly immovable, the flat of his hand coming up instead to stem the progress of the wood. Calmly, without haste, he stepped into the hallway, closing them both inside. To Deanna, faced all at once with his tall, arrogant male presence, the narrow passageway seemed to have shrunk to minuscule proportions.

'Bangs on the head should be taken seriously,' he advised her with cool precision, 'and I prefer to satisfy myself that all is truly well.' He walked along the hall towards her living-room, leaving her to follow in a state of fretful agitation.

'I've already said, I'm perfectly all right. You really don't have to stay,' she told him again.

'I insist,' he murmured. 'Making sure of your well-being is the least I can do when I am living next door. That is what good neighbours are for, is it not?'

The faint tilting of his mouth did absolutely nothing to soothe her troubled spirits. Having him as her neighbour only added to her feelings of disquiet, as well he knew.

His glance went around the sitting-room, skimming over the wide, buttoned couch and its scattering of velvet cushions, the two heaving bookshelves, with their well thumbed volumes, the Indian rugs which added a touch of luxury. The pictures on the wall caught his attention, wild, primitive scenes, captured in oils, and he stared at them for some moments.

'So this is where you spend your leisure time away from the Centre,' he mused thoughtfully, 'when you are not catering to distressed animals. I am very much interested in your home, Deanna. It reflects the essential *you*, the part of your personality that you keep hidden beneath that outer shell of cool porcelain. It is intriguing; there are great depths yet to be fathomed. We should talk, I think.'

'Tomorrow,' she said quickly. 'We could talk tomorrow, since you're intent on staying around. It's getting late, and I was actually thinking of going to bed.' As soon as she had said it, she recalled the words he had spoken to her in his own home, the anticipation of the pleasure it would give him to take her to bed, and she wished fervently that she had kept quiet. That he too recollected last evening was devastatingly clear from the way his mouth grooved, and his deeply golden gaze slanted over her. She was immediately reminded of the flimsy state of her attire, the thin silk gown that concealed none of her rounded curves, but in fact, she realised despairingly, served only to accentuate them. She ran trembling fingers along the embroidered overlap at her waist, as though the action would be some kind of shield.

'It is not that late,' he contradicted, his eyes assessing her slowly, with warm intimacy. 'The bang on your head must indeed have taken its toll if you are retiring so early. But it need not be a problem, you know, because I believe I can be of some help. There is a technique I have learned, a way of giving massage to relieve the points of tension that arise within the body. You will find it relaxing, I am sure.' He walked over to the couch. 'You must lie down, and I will show you how easily the pain will fade.'

'N-no.' The strangled word was dragged from her. The very thought of him laying hands on her sent her mind into a feverish spin. 'I really don't think that would be a good idea. You must go... please.'

He cast her a doubtful look, his glance returning to the couch. 'How can you dismiss something without even giving it a try? All you have to do is lie back, stretched out along the couch, and I will stand at this end—see, I will move this small table out of the way——' He bent towards the low table where she had pushed the parcel in her haste, and from the sudden stiffening of his body she knew that her worst fears had come to fruition. He had seen the gold vessels.

Words would not come from her throat. When she needed to speak, to explain, she could only stand and watch him slowly examine the contents of the box. Anger was etched into his hard-boned face as he turned around and fixed her with eyes that burned into her soul with the agonising thrust of hot steel.

'Now I see,' he said in a voice threaded with raw savagery, 'why you were so anxious for me to be gone.' His gaze seared her to the bone, filled her with dread.

'They... they are real, then?' she said haltingly. 'Not fakes?'

'As if you did not know. I was right in my very first supposition; you have been working with him all along, setting up this vile conspiracy.'

'No,' she blurted in sharp denial. 'It isn't true; it isn't what you think.'

Her shaken response had the opposite effect to that which she had wanted. It was like the spark that set the touch-paper alight, fanning the flames of his anger, rousing him to menacing fury. Fulminating rage sharply delineated the strong bones of his face, swept dark shadows along the planes and angles of those commanding, autocratic features, and Deanna was suddenly afraid, more afraid than she had ever been before.

'You would deny these vessels belong to me? Do you imagine I cannot recognise that which is mine? What kind of fool do you take me for?' The questions were shot at her with explosive force, an aggressive volley directed towards her in a wrathful, threatening blast, so that she took a step backwards.

'I didn't s-say that,' she managed in jerky retaliation. 'You're jumping to conclusions again...forming opinions about me without giving me the chance to explain.'

'What explanation can there be?' he ground out. Lifting one of the heavy pots from its wrapping, he held it up so that the glittering jewels flashed like sparks of flame in the lamplight. 'There are no others of their kind. These were part of my collection and now they are in your possession. They were stolen from me,' he said in a blistering indictment, 'and that makes you nothing more than a common thief. For this——' he pushed the gold vessel towards her with barely contained fury '—for *this* you would barter your soul?'

'You're wrong.' She struggled to keep her nerves steady under the onslaught of his scorching anger. 'I didn't steal them from you. Please don't think that.'

A muscle jerked along the angular sweep of his jaw. Placing the pot back in its box, he said through his teeth, 'I will not have these meaningless denials. You played the golden innocent from the moment we met, when all the time the truth was that you have the heart of an infidel. You have betrayed me, worked against me from the very beginning.' His mouth moved in a hard, contemptuous line. 'What was your plan for the future—to meet your worthless lover and share out the spoils?' His hands clenched into fists, flexing at his sides. 'It is over, finished,' he rasped, starting to move swiftly towards her. 'Understand? There is nothing left for you with him.'

She flinched as he approached, but managed to stay where she was. 'I know this looks bad,' she said, her throat tightly constricted, 'but you must believe me, I had nothing to do with the removal of your property, and I'm sure Luis had no intention of stealing from you. He is my dearest friend; he couldn't——'

He cut her off with an incredulous, angry breath of sound. 'You would still protect him? *Por Dios*! What hold does this man have over you, that you rush to defend him at every turn, that you risk your life by driving off towards the jungle at a moment's notice?'

'I just know,' she said unevenly, 'that you are wrong about him. He——'

'Your loyalty to this man offends me,' he bit out harshly. 'He dazzles you with the lure of his illicit plunder, he turns your head with feats of criminality that would outrage any sane and reasonable man, and you chase after him like a pathetic, lovelorn kitten.'

His hard, derisive tone lashed her, striking at the very core of her being, and she turned on him with a flare of angry rebellion. 'Don't talk about him in that way. I won't have it, do you hear? I won't listen to you saying such things.'

'You will listen,' he muttered with a deep, guttural inflexion, 'and you will learn that I am not to be trifled with. You risked everything for this man and the wealth he promised you, but all that is done with now.' His fingers curled around her throat, and her eyes widened in alarm at the primitive force which drove him.

'Alejo,' she whispered, 'please, you must hear what I have to say——' She choked back a gasp as his thumb began to brush slowly along the silken smoothness of her skin, setting up shock-waves of primal response that had nothing at all to do with the chaotic reasoning of her brain.

'You have said enough, more than enough,' he intoned with grim emphasis. 'I will wipe him from your mind. His existence in your life will be as the merest insect that flits past your head, here one moment, then gone forever. You do not need him, you do not need his paltry offerings—why would you chase a rainbow, when what you are searching for is close to hand?' His voice thickened, dropped to a low, persuasive growl. 'Play the game a different way, my cool, tantalising *Inglesa*, and watch the treasure trove pool at your feet.'

'Alejo,' she said huskily, 'you don't understand. It isn't the money——'

'That is what you said before,' he muttered with brittle impatience, 'yet you have in your room just one small portion of my own wealth. Your actions give the lie to your words, Deanna, but perhaps there is something more that drives you to follow him.' Anger sparked once more in his eyes. 'I do not believe it is love. You cannot love this man who has deserted you, or you would not have responded to me in such a way last night. He will be easily driven from your mind. I shall do it,' he asserted with superb arrogance. 'I shall make you forget him, because no matter what you have done there is a fire in me that burns for you, and I shall not rest until I have possessed you, until the flames are quenched.' He stared at her, passionate intensity warring with accusation. 'You have done this to me.'

He moved then, tilting her head back with his thumb, and his firm mouth claimed hers, crushing the protest that formed on her lips, and burning a trail of flame along the softly vulnerable contours, as though he would make her accept his challenge, devour her with the storm of his possessive demand. Fever spiralled in her, mounting like the turbulent shift of heat before a tropical storm. She wanted him, wanted his kisses, and the knowledge shamed her; even as her mind sent out frantic warnings she knew it, recognised that he kissed her with cold, angry passion born of contempt, and yet she could not push him away. Her strength failed her, blitzed by the warm, determined quest of his mouth, drained by the overwhelming intensity of her own need. Weakness invaded her limbs, and she clung to him for support, her fingers twisting against the thin material of his shirt. She felt the heat of his skin through the fine silk, the heavy thud of his heartbeat against his ribcage.

'*Te quiero*,' he said in a low growl against her hot cheek. 'I want you. That is how it has been from the first moment I set eyes on you. Desire for you runs like molten lava through my blood. I will have you,' he promised with ragged intent; 'I will make you mine, Deanna *mia*.'

A fleeting glimmer of caution surfaced in her and she tried to draw back. 'No,' she whispered, 'no. Not like this—Alejo——'

'*Si*, like this.' With compelling pressure, he dragged her to him, his hand in the small of her back, splayed out along her spine, drawing her slender, curving shape against his hard male body, so that she registered with mind-shattering thoroughness every rigid muscle, every tough sinew. Thoughts of resistance fled as she knew a wild and reckless urge to wrap herself around him, to fit her softness to every strong, masculine contour.

The hand at her throat slid down to mould the rounded slope of her shoulder, to knead with slow, sensuous movements that had a disastrous effect on her self-control. 'You have inflamed me,' he muttered thickly. 'I want to look at you, taste you, know every part of you.'

His lips made a fiery detour along the column of her throat, and she gave a deep, shuddery sigh. She was captivated by the slow sweep of his mouth on her sensitised skin, by the way his hands moved over her in a subtle caress, seeking out her slender shape. Each delicate brush of those knowing fingers left in its wake a tingling, thrilling rush of heat that was almost too much to bear.

'Alejo,' she mumbled abstractedly, her lips making a soft collision with the slightly roughened texture of his cheek as he lifted his head. Her limbs melted at the startling contact, her tongue flickered across his warm skin with involuntary need to taste and explore. He took her mouth again, nudging her lips apart, tasting the sweet inner recesses that had been denied him, and her hands crept up around his neck, her fingers tangling in the dark, crisp hair at his nape.

'You want me too,' he affirmed huskily. His hands were shifting over the vulnerable expanse from throat to shoulder, creating ripples of shivery excitement that ran along her heated flesh. She looked up at him, her eyes dazed with bewildered pleasure and mingled uncertainty, and he murmured, '*Sí*, it is true.' Her low gasp of protest went unheeded as he slid his thumbs beneath the edges of her robe, and pushed the silky constriction from her shoulders. 'Exquisite,' he breathed thickly, drawing the robe aside and letting his brilliant gaze ride a shimmering path over the smooth swell of her breasts, which were confined only by a delicate wisp of lace. 'You are as I imagined, *perfección*.'

He bent his head and tested the creamy slopes with lips and tongue, dipping to nuzzle each aroused crest through its flimsy covering, until every fibre of her being was suddenly concentrated on that sweet and shockingly sensuous friction. With every slow, gratifying flick of his tongue he was deepening the spell, working his strange enchantment until there could be no escape.

Her fingers jerked spasmodically against the hard muscles of his arms. 'How can you do this to me?' she whispered, stricken by her own inability to break away from this drugging ravishment of her senses. 'You don't even like me. No matter what I say, you think badly of me; you have no faith in my words or my feelings——'

'I want you,' he repeated bleakly. 'What you have done does not alter this fact.' She felt the tension in his body, the firm glide of his hands as they moved over her slender shape and came to rest on the warm curve of hip and thigh. Pulling her against him, he let her know the hard urgency of his need, while his mouth sought to plunder once again the tender, satiny arch of her throat. She moved convulsively against the sweet invitation of that intimate pressure, the ache within her growing as he thrust against her, her fingers clenching on the magnificent spread of his shoulders, feeling the flexing of his strong muscles with passionate delight.

'You are driving me crazy,' he growled against her skin; 'you push me to the very edge of insanity, but you will not win. I will have you, and that will be an end to it.'

Desperately she tried to summon up a vestige of will-power. She had to stop this. She couldn't give in to her pulsing, surging need. He hated her, he thought the very worst of her, and his urgent desire to possess her was nothing more than a bittersweet compulsion that would fade away as soon as he had sated himself with her. She couldn't bear to be used that way. She wanted him, she wanted his caresses, the honeyed rapture of his kisses, but not at such a price... only with love. The errant thought, slipping in on a hot tide of restless yearning, made her pulse flutter wildly. Love. Was that what she felt for him? A silent wail started up inside her and echoed around the desolate wastes of her heart. How could she have fallen for a man whose one thought was to use her for his own ends, who sought her out only in order to attain his true goal, to seize Luis and bring him to book?

Her body stiffened in tortured rejection. There was only pain in loving him, because there could be no answering fulfilment. He would never love her in return. Pride must come to her rescue, prevent her from submitting shamefully to his ruthless treatment of her. 'You can't do this,' she insisted, trying to inject a degree of coldness into her voice.

'Later,' he said, brushing his lips across the flushed pink of her cheek. 'Tell me later what it is I must not do.'

Her palms flattened against the hard wall of his chest, pushing him away. 'I mean what I say,' she told him. 'I don't care how inflamed your feelings are—I don't share them.'

His eyes narrowed on her, their message ominous. 'You are a liar,' he intoned softly. 'I feel you tremble in my arms, I feel your lips soften beneath mine, and I see for myself the evidence of your response——' His gaze flicked with slow insolence over her swollen breasts, their taut peaks even now chafing against the restriction of lace, and hot colour rose instantly, washing across her cheeks in a burning tide.

'That was unfair,' she breathed, hating her treacherous body, hating him even more for pointing it out.

'I am in no mood to be fair,' he said, his mouth twisting in recognition of his scoring thrust. 'You have hardly done anything to ease my own discomfort. Just the opposite, in fact.' He pushed her away from him, and Deanna quickly drew the folds of her robe around herself in a protective gesture which brought a febrile glitter to his eyes.

She turned and walked over to the small table, putting some small distance between them. He had allowed her to get away from him, and she must do what she could with this breathing space to repair the damage and bring things down to a less heated level. How, though, how was she to begin?

Her glance went to the gold pots, nestling in their box, and she drew in a deep breath and said, 'These were sent to me just this afternoon. You saw Carmela give me the parcel, didn't you?' She raised questioning eyes to him, and he inclined his head briefly in acknowledgement.

'That is true, though it does not necessarily signify——'

'It signifies,' she said, her lips firming, 'that they weren't in my possession until a few hours ago. There was no accompanying letter, and I've no idea why they've come to me, but I'm sure that as soon as Luis comes back he will explain everything to your satisfaction.'

His dark brows lifted. 'You are so sure that he is coming back?' he queried drily.

She ignored the scepticism in his tone and went on, 'Perhaps there was something wrong, something in your own household that prevented him from returning them to you. I don't know, I can only guess.' She held out his valuables to him, but he made no effort to retrieve them, only viewed her thoughtfully. 'Please take them,' she persisted. 'I don't think I ever want to see them again.'

'*Gracias*,' he said, his mouth a hard, unyielding line as he took the box she offered. Still he watched her with that dark, unreadable expression, and she thought unhappily that she was nearing the end of her tether with his doubt and cynicism. Any more and she would be at breaking-point.

'Will you go now?' she pressed, her voice strained.

'*De acuerdo*. There is nothing more, I think, to be achieved this night, and so I shall leave you to your... lonely bed.' He smiled grimly. 'I shall see you in the morning, no doubt.'

A tiny, jagged line worked its way into her brow. 'I dare say you will,' she muttered. From the barely hidden threat that underlay his cool manner, it seemed that he was still intent on following her every move, and that gave her an even bigger headache than she had experienced earlier.

Impassively, he studied her harassed expression. '*Buenas noches*, Deanna,' he murmured.

CHAPTER SEVEN

LETHARGY and unease hung close and clouded Deanna's mind all through the next morning. She had not slept well. Why had her feelings for Alejo crystallised in such an unhappy fashion? Love had no place in their relationship, now or in the future, for he would never look on her with anything other than want and need and a desire to reach his one true objective, Luis. The night had been filled with troubled dreams, hopes and fantasies that she knew could never be fulfilled, that only left her exhausted.

It was madness to let thoughts of Alejo invade her being this way, when his only intention was to possess her and rid himself of unwanted feverish desire. She must cast aside these draining emotions which only left her feeling increasingly miserable, and force herself instead to concentrate on what she had to do.

Luis had asked her to go to him, and she must set off on the road for the lodge as soon as was humanly possible. It seemed, though, that everything was conspiring against her, because by lunchtime she was still cooling her heels in the Centre. The key to the Centre's garage, where her pick-up had been locked away overnight, was missing, and since she had been able to find neither

Alejo nor Carmela she found herself wandering around in increasing frustration.

'Is your headache still troubling you?' Alejo asked, walking into the office just after lunch, and giving her a carefully assessing look.

Her pulses leapt into frantic action at his approach. He looked cool and in control, his crisp black hair gleaming in the rays of golden sunlight that filtered through the windows, his casual but expensive clothes emphasising the breadth of shoulder and the lean, hard-muscled thighs. Cream-coloured trousers moulded his strong limbs, a white, finely striped shirt beneath the cream jacket enhanced the masculine perfection of his powerful chest.

Her glance skittered away. 'I'm fully recovered, thank you,' she answered stiffly. 'But I would have been much easier in my mind if I'd been able to find the key to the garage. Do you have it? I tried your apartment earlier but it seemed you were out.'

'I was. There were a few urgent matters I had to attend to.' He studied her, his dark eyes busy taking in the softly flowing lines of her cotton dress, the slender arch of her feet in the white leather sandals. 'The key, though, is out of commission at the moment, as I am having a duplicate made. Was there some problem?'

'I should have thought the problem was obvious,' she said grittily, chafing beneath the thoroughness of his appraisal and aggravated by the way things were turning out. She did not want to have to explain herself and her actions to him, yet it was increasingly obvious that there was to be no escape. 'I've some deliveries to make later this afternoon, and I shall need the pick-up.' If yesterday was anything to go by, he would leave her little chance of slipping away unnoticed, and she might as well face the situation head-on. If he showed signs of following her, she would have to do what she could to throw him off the trail, perhaps lead him on a roundabout journey, until she could finally lose him. After an hour or two of genuine deliveries, he would surely lose interest.

'Ah, the truck,' he murmured. 'I noticed that there was some slight problem with one of the tyres after your unfortunate skid yesterday. It will be dealt with later.'

'I didn't notice anything wrong,' she said with a frown. 'And anyway, if it's only slight, it won't matter greatly; I could still use it.'

'That is completely out of the question,' he stated firmly. 'I could not for one moment sanction such a hazardous venture.'

Deanna's gaze shot over him in growing frustration as she thought around the problem. He was doing this deliberately, she was convinced, and all her arguments would fall on stony ground. If only she could confide in him—but Luis had said his life was in danger, and she dared not take the risk. 'When she comes in, I'll ask Carmela if she will loan me her vehicle,' she said. She couldn't afford to let him thwart her every move, not with Luis wounded and needing her.

'Carmela will not be able to do that, I am afraid,' he told her, not sounding the least bit regretful. 'She has some calls of her own to make, and I understand that they will take up most of the day.'

Deanna had the strongly intuitive feeling that he had had a large hand in engineering those calls, and the thought that he could run circles around her like this was adding to her restlessness more and more with each minute that passed.

'There really is no need to let this situation disturb you so greatly,' Alejo said, watching her as he placed his own keys in the cupboard and then shrugged out of his jacket. 'My vehicle is at your disposal, though of course it would be better if I drive you wherever you wish to go, since you are unused to the controls. It will be no great trouble to me to accompany you on your delivery rounds, since I wish anyway to become more acquainted with the day-to-day business of the Centre. You can explain to me the various aspects of your work.'

'Carmela would be much better suited to that task,' Deanna answered in a clipped tone, recognising his barely disguised determination to stay close by her wherever she went. 'She's worked here longer than I have, and she knows all there is to know about the running of the Centre. Besides,' she added with an inner pang, 'you two get on so well together, I am sure she'll be delighted to have your company when she makes her calls today.'

'What is this?' Carmela asked, coming into the room. 'Are you coming with me, Alejo? How wonderful. Now, if you could return the favour, next time you go to the States,' she added with a cheeky grin, 'I should love to come along.' She sobered quickly. 'Amend that. I should not enjoy the journey at all, for I hate to fly, you know. It is a phobia. But my family are there, and my mother is not well.'

'It will be my pleasure to take you, Carmela. You should have mentioned it before this.' Alejo put his arm around the girl. 'When your mother has the operation, she will be much better, you know. It will not be long now, I imagine. Do you have an exact date?'

Carmela nodded, and Deanna watched in mute misery as Alejo hugged her close. Why could she not share with him such a warm, easy affection? Her own body pulsed with longing for his touch, but it was forbidden fruit; there were too many dangers in leaving herself openly vulnerable to this man. Watching her friend glide into his embrace was a refined torture. She liked Carmela, and she was sorry about her mother, but the sight of the beautiful girl wrapped up in Alejo's arms made her feel totally wretched. It just went to show how right she had been to accept his lovemaking for what it really was—the opportunist move of a man who could go from one woman to another without a qualm.

'I will show you the letter she wrote to me—if you would like to see it?' Carmela's gaze lifted in unconscious appeal, and Alejo responded with a quick smile.

'Of course. Does she tell you a little more about what is to be done?'

'Yes, but I am not sure I understand fully. You might see better what is involved, though.' She clasped her fingers in a tense little gesture. 'It was so good of you to arrange all this with the surgeon, Alejo.'

He squeezed her gently. 'It was nothing. Your mother is a very dear friend of my own mother. It is the very least I could do for her. Now, where is this letter?'

'It's in the other office,' Carmela said. 'Come through with me, and I will find it.'

Silently, Deanna blessed Carmela for the diversion. Alejo had quite casually placed his keys in the cupboard, confident, no doubt, that the ones she needed had been removed, but this was all the chance she wanted to set off for the lodge without him. The use of his own vehicle was an offer he had made tongue in cheek, not believing for one moment that she would take him up on it. He was mistaken. It was only his services as driver that she would decline.

Lifting the keys from the hook, she hurriedly collected together the things she needed and went outside to the Range Rover. At the door, she paused, uncertain as an indistinct tremor seemed to shake the ground beneath her feet. Looking back towards the buildings of the Centre, she could see only the slightest vibration of shutters, nothing more, and she decided that she could not let the warning rumblings of nature deflect her from her purpose.

The door was unlocked, and after a moment or two of searching she found the key she needed and fitted it into the ignition. Nothing happened. Try as she might, she could not turn it to spark the engine into life.

'*A donde va usted?*' Alejo's terse query sent ripples of quivery apprehension shooting along her nervous system. 'Where are you going?' he repeated, his sharp glance moving over her stricken features in taut censure.

Her mouth was suddenly very dry. 'You said,' she answered in husky explanation, 'that your vehicle was at my disposal. I'm merely taking you up on that offer. I'm sure I shall cope quite well once I get started—there really is no need for you to put yourself to any trouble on my account.'

'It is no trouble,' he assured her grimly. 'You will move over to the passenger seat, *por favor*.' As he climbed into the front seat alongside her, the pressure of his hard frame and the firm hand on her arm gave her little choice but to do as he requested. His gaze skimmed the interior and came to rest on the package of antibiotics. 'I see we are to make the same delivery as yesterday,' he said. '*Está bien*. I believe I know the way.' Releasing the steering lock and starting up the engine, he swung the Range Rover out on to the road. 'The only difficulty,' he continued as they gathered speed, 'is in knowing which lodge he has chosen for his refuge. I will take a guess, and make for the nearest, but you will correct me if I am wrong. You would not want your *amigo's* suffering to be prolonged any more than is necessary, would you?' He absorbed her strangled gulp and the pained darkening of her blue eyes with evident satisfaction. 'No. It is as I thought, we are going in the right direction.'

Tension coiled in her like a tightly wound spring, and the shrill cry of a bird wheeling overhead made her jerk in her seat, her fingers clenching on the smooth upholstery as though it were some kind of lifeline. A faint film of perspiration broke out on her forehead, not solely due to the heat and humidity of the day. Her reactions did not go unnoticed.

'You should learn to relax,' he cautioned with dry, cruel humour, throwing her an oblique glance as he moved to change gear to accommodate the increasing ruggedness of the terrain. 'We have some distance to travel, and if you are going to hug your seat like that for the whole of the journey you will be black and blue by the time we arrive at our destination.'

How could she relax? How could she ever forgive herself, when her own foolhardy actions were taking him every moment closer to Luis? With each passing mile the jungle grew nearer, the luxuriant vegetation encroaching on the dusty road, the trees taller, wound about with creepers and vivid blossoms that provided a brilliant splash of colour against the spreading green leaves.

'As you said, your idea of my travel plans is purely guesswork, and so is your presumption about who my deliveries are intended for,' she returned with an effort, struggling to take a firm hold on herself. 'And I don't see the need for you to accompany me everywhere I go, simply to satisfy a passing curiosity in the nature of my work.'

'This pretence is no longer necessary,' he informed her curtly. 'I know full well the plans that have been hatching in your head, and since it is clear that you have chosen to totally ignore my warnings of yesterday I shall take matters into my own hands. Regardless of the dangers that abound in this area for a woman untried and alone, you are set on rushing to your lover's side. So be it. I shall be there with you when you greet him, or you will not greet him at all.'

Deanna's fingers curled tightly in her lap. He was warning her of danger? As far as she was concerned, there was far more danger inherent in being thrown into close proximity to this man, who could, by a look or gesture, cause an alarming rise in her temperature and an equally hectic disturbance to her pulse-rate. It wouldn't do to let him get the upper hand. He could destroy her in the process.

'I won't allow you to dictate terms to me,' she vowed with asperity. 'You're making too many assumptions, among them the idea that you can act as my shadow. You must turn this vehicle around at once and let me continue my work on my own, under my own terms.'

'Your show of spirit is admirable, *gatita*, but it will avail you nothing. Besides,' he added, turning off towards the rutted track that led towards the lodge, 'you may find that you are only too glad of my company if your lover is ill. How will you manage a sick man by yourself?' His glance shifted over her. 'You are so slender, lovely to look at and perfectly shaped, but not, I think, strong enough to cope with a man who is helpless and who may need lifting.' His expression hardened. 'You must admit defeat in this. I am with you, we are going to find him together, there is nothing you can do to stop it. I am surprised that you would even try, since now we have both seen the evidence of his treachery.'

Deanna watched the diamond-hard glitter form in his dark eyes and felt a shudder of dismay rack her body. He would show no mercy. It was as Luis had said: he was ruthless, and she was powerless to stop him.

'Would you convict a man without a fair trial?' she asked huskily. 'You haven't heard yet what he has to say about his actions.' Why hadn't she been able to keep Luis's secret? She had failed him. It was only because of her persistence in setting out on this mission that Alejo was with her now, and everything that Luis feared would come to pass.

'Do not berate yourself, Deanna,' he instructed harshly. 'From the moment I set eyes on you, your lover's future was assured. Nothing you could do, or say, would have changed the turn of events.'

'He's not my lover.' Her whispered words seemed to echo in the charged silence that fell between them.

His eyes narrowed on her, his intake of breath barely perceptible. 'Is this yet another ploy? Explain yourself,' he demanded with cold arrogance.

'We met years ago,' she said, 'when my mother and father came to live in Peru. Our parents were friendly with each other, and we mixed in the same circles so that Luis and I were always together. We became almost inseparable.' She glanced quickly at Alejo, and found that he was scowling darkly, his attention fixed on the rough road ahead.

'You were inseparable. I see. This does not convince me that there is nothing lover-like in his behaviour towards you. Or have I missed the point?'

His cool derision made jagged inroads on her already fractured nerves. She said hastily, 'I meant to say that he was like a brother to me.'

'Indeed. How charming. And I suppose you will have me also believe that when you were older there was never anything between you, he never once so much as kissed you?'

Her colour fluctuated as she thought of the few kisses they had shared, those first stumbling forays of youthful passion, and the coldness of his expression settled into ice.

'As I thought. Lying does not suit you; your fine English complexion gives you away too easily.'

'What I'm telling you is the truth,' she insisted. 'If I want to protect Luis, it's because he is like a brother to me, because I believe implicitly in his honour.'

He waved aside her protestations. 'It is no longer of any importance,' he said tersely. 'We are here now, and perhaps we may begin to get at the real facts underlying this situation.'

She saw with a jolt that it was as he said. The wooden lodge had come into view, set high on its wide-based stilts, a solid-looking building, despite its abandonment by the scientists.

He stopped the vehicle and came around to the passenger side to help her out. As his large fingers circled her arm in a firm grip, she placed her small hand over his own and looked at him in quick desperation. She said urgently, 'You will listen to what he has to say, won't you? You won't harm him? He's sick, he——'

'And you say that this man is not your lover?' His gaze lashed her with contempt. 'Yet you plead for him, your lips tremble for him, your blue, blue eyes are filled with anguish for his plight.' Deep anger tightened the lines of his mouth, added steel hardness to the line of his jaw as he pushed her away from him. Deanna saw it, and her mind filled with horror at what she had inadvertently done, with the knowledge that somehow she had made matters worse.

'He's a good man; I've known him for so long, he's always been open with me, told me everything.'

'But you profess not to know anything about these latest events, the reasoning behind the theft of my belongings?' His tone was glacial as he moved towards the steps of the lodge, and the door which hung loose on its hinges.

She could only shake her head miserably. 'He said there was danger, and that it was best for my own sake that I didn't know anything.'

He pushed the door to one side and looked swiftly around. Deanna, following close behind, gazed in at the empty room.

'It looks,' he said, 'as though we are once again too late. Our friend has gone.'

She stared at him. 'But he can't have gone. He asked me to come—he needed my help. He must have been in some terrible danger to have left without seeing me.' Fear struck her, whitening her face. 'He said he was being followed,' she muttered; 'that men were coming after him, and that his life was in danger. He has already been wounded.' Her voice sank to a desperate whisper. 'What can have happened?'

'Wounded?' he repeated, in a harsh echo of sound. His face set in lines of taut anger that made her heartbeat quicken. 'How can you have been so reckless,' he gritted, 'so heedless of your own safety, to come out here, knowing full well that he was being followed by men capable of such acts? Did you not stop for one moment to consider the complete and utter folly of your actions, the risk to yourself if these men had found you?'

She stared at him, nonplussed. 'I had to come,' she reasoned shakily. 'He needed me. He thought this place would be a refuge; he believed he had lost them, and he asked for my help and I—I failed him...' Her voice trailed away miserably.

'Calm yourself.' It was a brusque command, accompanied by the lacerating edge of his steel-eyed glance. 'Your behaviour defies understanding. Not only have you missed death by inches in racing at breakneck speed along a mud track, it now transpires that it is by sheer fortune alone that you have not fallen into the hands of brigands or worse.'

'But I——'

'Do not throw at me any more of your excuses,' he cut in, his tone blistering. 'I think I shall not be responsible for my actions if you persist.' He moved away from her, his dark gaze slanting over the clearing. 'I believe from all the signs around here that the danger in being in this place may be past. There are two sets of tracks, which must indicate that these men have already been and gone.'

Her breath caught in an agonised gasp. 'Then—you think that they've found him?' She sent a searching, despairing glance over the furrowed earth.

'No. From all appearances, one set of tracks must have been made earlier, and there is no sign of a scuffle. It looks rather as though Luis San Martin fled the coop just in time.'

'But——'

'As to his needing your help,' he said dismissively, 'that is debatable. It may be, however, that he has left some clue inside as to where he is headed, some clue that you and no other might be able to interpret. Again, it is guesswork, but it will do no harm to search. In the morning, we can go after him.'

He walked into the main room of the lodge, and Deanna, following him, moistened her dry lips with the tip of her tongue. 'In the morning?' she questioned him huskily. 'If he's hurt, then that might be too late.'

'Nothing will be served by going after him tonight. Already darkness is falling, and the territory is unsafe. The morning will suffice, and we shall be safe enough here for the night.'

Her gaze locked with his. 'You mean we're staying?'

'Of course. It has been a long drive and it would be foolish to go any further now.'

Deanna's stomach lurched in agonised acceptance, acknowledging the truth in what he said. Even so, she pressed on haltingly, 'But he may not be far away. There might be something I could do, if only I could find him in time.'

'Enough.' His tone was sharp, brooking no argument. 'Your persistence is beginning to annoy me. Some hours ago I might have vented my spleen on San Martin for coaxing you out here to face unknown perils, but now I am seeing for myself that more likely he would have encountered trouble in keeping you away.' He sent her a fierce glower. 'I will not have you stumbling around in the undergrowth for this man. Besides which, it would be pointless. Even from the most cursory glance around here, it is clear that there are no signs of very recent occupation, and he is most likely long gone. Go and make yourself useful and see if you can light the stove. At least we shall have a drink after our journey. I shall bring in blankets.'

He started back out of the door, and Deanna said frowningly, 'Blankets? Do you keep them in your vehicle?'

His mouth moved in a tight line. 'Only when I am expecting to come on a journey such as this, with an impetuous, headstrong young woman. I have brought provisions, too. We shall not starve.'

She swallowed. He had known all along what she would attempt to do. It was almost as though he had led her into it, baited the trap and then watched it close around her.

Shivering, despite the heat, she walked into the lodge and looked around more closely at her surroundings. Surprisingly, there was no aura of neglect, but instead everything appeared clean and neat, and the furnishings, though simple, were serviceable and adequate. Perhaps whoever was responsible for the lodge kept it in good condition in case it should be brought into use some time in the future.

She, like Alejo, could see little evidence of Luis's recent occupation, and for a while she began to doubt that he had ever been here. It was only when she glanced into a waste-bin and saw, beside a couple of tins which had clearly been rinsed out, a blood-soaked cloth, that her heart contracted in anguish. Why hadn't she been able to get here sooner? She wished she knew how he had been hurt. Forgery was big business, Alejo had said, and the men involved were without scruples. A shudder rippled through her at the thought of guns, and her mind shied away from all the implications.

'I see that you too thought to bring along some essentials,' Alejo said, placing a box of supplies on the large wooden table that stood in the centre of the room. A crumpled piece of paper lay on its surface, and he pushed it to one side. 'That is good. We have water as well,' he added, going outside again and returning in a short while with a large canister which he stood beside the box. 'Did you manage to get the stove working?'

'Oh——' Flustered, Deanna tried to bring her thoughts back to the matter in hand. 'I haven't looked at it yet. I'll do it now.'

He glanced at her narrowly, but said nothing as he unpacked the cans of food and boxes of dried milk. Picking up the paper, he opened it out and scanned it quickly. 'This is, I think, meant for you.'

Turning, she studied him blankly for a moment, then reached for the paper with trembling fingers. Her name, and a date, nothing more. Puzzled, she stared at it, then looked up at Alejo. His dark eyes were shuttered, revealing nothing of his inner thoughts, but he knew, he must know, that it was a message, a clue to Luis's whereabouts, and he would wait, biding his time until he discovered the secret.

'I don't know what it means,' she said helplessly. 'I just can't think——'

'You are tired, and distraught. Later, when you have eaten, and you are rested, the meaning will become clear to you. Come, we will prepare this meal together. It will be quicker that way.'

His cool, commanding presence did a lot to settle her nerves. She had not expected to feel grateful to him, but his quiet, firm assurance registered on her senses and had a remarkably soothing effect. With him, she felt safe, secure, as though he was a bulwark against adversity.

They ate without talking, yet the silence did not seem oppressive, and Alejo did nothing to break it. She was busy with her thoughts, mulling over the date written on that crumpled piece of paper. What had happened in that distant year? Where had she been? Where had Luis been? A flicker of remembrance crossed her mind, an image of the village where he'd once lived, up in the hills, and Alejo murmured shrewdly, 'You have solved the mystery?'

'I...I'm not sure.' With all her heart, she wished that she could trust him and confide in him her thoughts, but what did she really know about him? For all that it seemed like a lifetime, she had known him for just a short while, and already she had seen in him the ruthlessness and determination that lay at the core of his being. Luis's warning sounded in the back of her mind, compounding her fears, and, though instinct was telling her to cast that particular counselling to one side and follow the urgings of her innermost self, another part of her was sounding the beat of caution. Luis's life was indeed endangered; that message had been driven home starkly in the sight of that blood-soaked bandage. Would it hasten his end if he was brought out of hiding and into the open to stand trial? Wouldn't he then be a sitting target for those who wanted to finish him off? It was a risk she dared not take.

'No? That is unfortunate,' he said, his voice gravel-harsh, and she looked at the astute shading of his features and felt the tension building in her once more.

The picture of an empty cottage was growing clearer in her mind with every minute, but how could she get to the village without Alejo knowing she had gone? Her only chance was to leave at first light, while he was sleeping, and make her way up into the hills.

He was watching her closely; she could feel his dark gaze fixed broodingly on her face, and she moved restlessly, gathering up her dishes and taking them over to the sink.

'I hope,' he growled, 'that you are not thinking of going after him alone.'

Apprehension rose in a swift wave as he came and stood beside her, but she did her best to stifle it. 'Whatever put that idea into your head?' she queried with an attempt at a negligent shrug.

'Do not play games with me, Deanna *mia*. Do you seriously believe that I cannot read your thoughts? Think again. I am beginning to know you very well, and I know when your mind is busy making plans. Forget them. You will not venture after him alone.'

'I didn't——' She broke off as the earth seemed to shift momentarily and she swayed, thrown into confusion by the unexpected movement. A faint rattling sound assaulted her ears, and she stared around, her eyes widening in alarm, a nervous shiver running along her spine and prickling the nape of her neck.

'It is the window blinds, nothing more,' Alejo said, winding his arms around her. 'It is over now, you see? Everything is still and there is no need to be afraid. You are quite safe.' The warmth of his large hands penetrated the thin fabric of her dress, heating her chilled flesh. A quivery breath shuddered in her throat, held back as she drank in the sweet comfort offered by his embrace.

'These tremors have been happening more and more frequently these last few days,' she said shakily, her fingers pressured lightly against his chest in tender confinement, registering the steady beat of his heart.

'*Tranquilo*, Deanna. We are used to them in these parts. Very occasionally, I believe, you have experienced similar disturbances in England, but here, in the lower-lying areas, there is little or no danger.' His hands gently kneaded her slender frame, so that she felt his calm strength seeping into her. 'Your recent troubles have left you overwrought,' he said, 'and these minor tremors are affecting you more deeply than they would in normal circumstances. They are something new and unknown to you, and that is why you fear them. You may rest easy. It is the more distant regions, the higher foothills, that are more likely to suffer any damage.'

Then Luis's village might be in danger—the horrifying thought settled on her mind like a black cloud. She would never know, unless she went after him.

Alejo's voice intruded on her thoughts once more. 'Most of the building work these days is done in what are considered safe regions. Does that not put your mind at rest?'

'I—yes, I suppose it does.' Once more she found herself wishing that she could confide in him and let his strength be her refuge.

'Come and sit down over here, with me,' he said, drawing her towards a blanket-covered divan which rested alongside one wall. 'I do not like to see you so upset, *enamorada*. Have faith in me, and let me do what I can to soothe away your troubles.' Pulling her down beside him, he tugged her into his arms, his long fingers warmly caressing the tense muscles of her shoulders, and the nape of her neck, until slowly the knots eased out and a slow wave of heat and a heavy lassitude began to spread throughout her body.

'How do you do that?' she mumbled. 'It feels so good, it makes me feel drowsy almost...' She twisted in his arms. 'What am I doing? I mustn't sleep, Alejo, I need to think.'

'You need do nothing,' he murmured. 'There have been enough trials and tribulations these last few days, and now it is time to forget them and conserve your strength. Relax.'

'I can't,' she said, 'I——'

His kiss stemmed the words, his mouth homing in on hers with bruising compulsion as though that was where it belonged, and her stunned senses recognised only the sweet, aching pleasure of a joy she had been denied too long. Her lips parted, yielding to the tender ravishment, seduced into feverish acquiescence by the warm probing of his tongue. The faint fragrance of musk clung to his skin, hung on the air between them, and she breathed it in raggedly, intoxicated by his closeness and the heat of his hard male body as he urged her back against the pillows.

'You see how easy it is?' he whispered thickly. 'Let me take your mind off your troubles. I shall kiss all your problems away.' Hungrily, he reached for her once more, feeding her own craving with the heated pressure of his hard mouth and the slow and sensuous glide of his tongue along the soft fullness of her lips.

Of their own volition, her fingers crept upwards and curled into the soft folds of his shirt, exploring with guilty delight the feel of hard, smooth muscle. A shuddery sigh ran through her. 'Why?' she muttered against the slightly roughened texture of his jaw. 'Why are you doing this to me? Is it some kind of punishment, some refined way of making me pay for the way you've been cheated?'

'What is this talk of punishment?' he intoned deeply, his hand making a fiery trail along her curving length. With humiliating eagerness, her body arched to meet the tantalising lure of that caress, her breasts swelling, becoming taut. 'Does this feel like punishment to you? If it does, then I must surely be doing something wrong.'

'Then does this mean . . . ?' She struggled against the heady enticement of his knowing hands, trying to quell the feverish stirrings of her blood that were rendering her thinking as nebulous as sea mist. 'Does this mean that you believed me when I said I had nothing to do with the theft? You were so angry, I thought——'

'What concern can I have for mere pots, empty vessels, when there is a treasure far more priceless to be pursued, *querida*? You are more precious than anything I have encountered before; your loveliness takes my breath away.' His hands moved to stroke the bright sheen of her curls, which spilled out in an unruly mass over the pillow, his fingers toying with the springy, vibrant tendrils. 'What gold can compare with the spun threads that run through my hands right at this moment?' he asked softly. 'There are no jewels to rival the sparkling blue depths of your eyes, or the rich, rosy flush of your lips. You are everything I ever dreamed of in a woman. I cannot think how I have lived so long without tasting such sweet golden perfection.'

'Alejo,' she mumbled huskily, 'I've been so unhappy about deceiving you, but I didn't know what to do for the best. You've been wronged, I know, but I can't change what has happened. I don't even understand it myself.'

'We shall forget it, push it to one side,' he pronounced fiercely. 'Put your arms around me, *querida*. Touch me, feel how my heart thunders with wanting you.' He leaned over her, his chest softly crushing her breasts, his mouth making a scorching detour along the vulnerable slope of her throat and dipping to trace the line of her bodice. 'This dress,' he murmured, 'is very pretty. I like it, you understand, but I should much rather see what is hidden beneath the beautiful wrapping.'

Her zip slid apart in his hands, the dress falling away from her before she had time to summon up any kind of resistance. He watched it slide to the floor with infinite satisfaction, then turned to look at her with heated intensity, the brilliant flame of desire burning deep in his eyes. She felt the crashing of his heart against his ribcage, and saw with startled, breathless wonder the faint trembling of his fingers as he dealt with the clasp of her lacy bra. 'Alejo, please,' she whispered in belated protest as her flimsy covering was tugged from her and she tried to cover her nakedness with her hands. Firmly he drew them away, his gaze sliding down to linger in absorbed fascination on the creamy swell of her breasts and the tightly furled pink crescents, before at last shifting to search her face. Hot colour washed over her cheeks.

'You are surely not embarrassed?' he queried in soft amazement. 'How can you be, when you are so incredibly lovely? How can you think of hiding such delights from me?' Her strangled reply was lost in the tender conquest he made of her mouth, and when his hands curved around the heavy fullness of her breasts she knew only a mindless desire to have more, to have all her secret dreams and fantasies fulfilled.

The lap of his tongue on the hard little buds was almost more than she could stand. Her fingers bit into the hardness of his shoulders, as she moved restively against that teasing ministration, provoked and enticed by it until the need inside her spiralled out of control and she cried out in confused and bewildered pleading for something unknown, for something her untutored body had no experience of.

His hands shifted over her, gliding smoothly along the silken sweep of her skin until the filmy barrier of her panties halted his progress. His lips followed the trail of his hands and with muttered impatience he slipped the last scrap of silk and lace from her. Her efforts to evade him, made in a last, fleeting bid for sanity, came to nothing as his hands returned to their gratifying voyage of discovery and she was melting, dissolving, her limbs fluid under the spellbinding enchantment of his stroking, gentle fingers. A low, aching sound of yearning surfaced in her throat as he found her moist centre, and with a shuddery sigh she abandoned all thought of denying his thrilling quest. A fire raged in her, the flames fanned by those seeking, circling fingers, and the cries broke from her, all the want and need focused in this sharp and sweetly stinging arousal.

'I know,' he whispered huskily against her scented skin. 'I know, *enamorada*, what it is that you want. Take it slowly, savour it.'

She could not take it slowly. She loved him and she wanted him, and the hard urgency of his superbly male body told her that he wanted her every bit as badly as she needed him. He shucked out of his clothes in a fluid, supple movement, and she stared at him in awe and wonderment, her fingers drawn to worship the smooth velvet of his skin as he came down to her once more. Her lips grazed the perfection of his chest, and she felt his muscles contract beneath the softness of her mouth. She looked at him again. He was bronzed and magnificent, flat-stomached and firm-muscled, and she felt a sudden quiver of nervousness that she wouldn't be able to please him, that he would find her lacking in some way.

'*Te quiero*,' he whispered roughly. Slowly he parted her thighs, the hard thrust of his manhood probing the heart of her femininity, and she stiffened, her body locking in sudden fear and uncertainty. He paused, frowning, his dark gaze sweeping her face. 'What is wrong?' he asked, his voice a rasping thread of sound. 'Have I frightened you?'

'N-no,' she said on a strangled note, her throat constricting as the urgency of his arousal tested the limits of her panicked control.

His body tensed as he stared down at her, his eyes growing wide and brilliant in shocked recognition. 'You have never—I did not know,' he muttered thickly, his breathing laboured. 'How could I have known...that this is your first time? All along, I believed——' He shook his head dazedly. 'You have never known a man before.' A surge of power, of bursting vitality rippled through his long, lean frame, and he claimed her lips with bruising intensity. 'I do not want to hurt you, *querida*,' he said fiercely, the words tumbling against her soft mouth, 'but—*perdición*—I do not think I can stop now.'

'I don't want you to stop,' she said raggedly. 'I want you; I want you so much, Alejo.'

'You are sure of this?' It was a strained, torn query.

'I'm sure.'

He kissed her again, stroking the heated centre of her femininity with tantalising sureness until she melted with pure, single-minded need. Only then did he thrust slowly into her with a heavy groan of satisfaction, absorbing her soft sigh of startled wonder with tender murmurings breathed against her cheek. He began to move, the controlled, rhythmic plunge of his body taking her with him to explore new heights of ecstasy and passion, sparking in her a wild, raging fire. She was soaring, the flames of excitement within her fanned by his passionate lovemaking until the blaze built to a zenith of pleasure, an incandescent and mind-shattering explosion of fulfilment. Her muscles clenched convulsively and his control finally broke, his own release coming within moments, his body shuddering, a harsh sound echoing in the cavern of his throat.

He wound his arms around her as the warm aftermath of their desire slowly ebbed away. 'I am honoured, Deanna *mia*, that you have made me this gift.' His breath feathered her hair as he brushed his lips over her heat-flushed cheeks, and he whispered softly, 'He was never your lover, this Luis San Martin. You have given yourself to me, and I am beyond words to express how that makes me feel.' His fingers traced a gentle path across her brow. 'Trust in me, Deanna *mia*, and I will take care of you. You have my promise. Your worries, your fears, your problems, they are mine from now on. I will deal with all of them.'

Held securely in the close circle of his arms, she pressed her lips to the smooth silk of his skin, but she could not prevent the tiny frown that etched its way into her brow.

'What is wrong? Tell me,' he insisted huskily. 'Are you thinking of San Martin? You need be anxious no more on his account. You know where he is, don't you? Tell me the name of his village, *querida*, and at first light tomorrow the end to your problems will be in sight.'

'There may be more earth tremors,' she said hesitantly. 'He used to live up in the hills in Trevillo—I'm afraid that it might be a dangerous journey, with the tremors increasing these last few days, but we must hope we can get there before there are any major quakes, and...before those other men can get to him.'

'I know the best routes through the hills,' he said firmly. 'Do not be concerned any longer, and try to get some sleep. The morning will come soon enough.'

Wrapped in his warm embrace, Deanna found it easy to follow his soft urging and let the tension flow from her. Her eyelids drooped wearily, her cheek cushioned by the smooth muscle of his chest, the steady thud of his heartbeat, the slow rise and fall of his breathing a drugging lullaby.

Some time in the night, the slumbrous melody began to fade, its rhythm undergoing a subtle change. Deanna stirred, waking slowly as sunlight angled in through the window blinds, and she sat up drowsily and looked around, her mind hazy and disorientated with sleep. The blinds were shaking; there was again that strange shifting of the earth that she had encountered before. She was naked beneath a thin covering blanket, and her body felt strange, as though she had a new awareness of herself. The events of the previous night came back to her in a warm flood of heat, and she turned slowly to look at Alejo, to feast her gaze on his familiar, darkly attractive features.

He was not with her in the bed, and she stood up carefully, wrapping the blanket around her as she went in search of him. The lodge, though, was quite empty, and when she went outside and looked around the clearing it too was desolate. Dismayed, she saw that the Range Rover had gone, and it finally dawned on her in a bleak and bitter realisation that she was totally and utterly alone. Alejo had accepted her trust, and then thrown it right back in her face. He had gone.

CHAPTER EIGHT

DEANNA stared around her blindly, unable to take in fully the extent of his betrayal. He would not simply have left her here, surely? There must be some other explanation, and he would be back at any moment to tell her that she was letting her imagination run riot. Of course he would be back.

The incredible folly of her thinking was borne in on her as time slowly passed and there was still no sign of his imminent return. Tears banked behind her eyelids and she dashed them away with the back of her hand. Why had he done this to her? Had last night meant nothing more to him than a one-night liaison with a woman he had briefly desired? Perhaps he had found her inexperience tedious, and his interest in her had waned disastrously. How could she have been so stupid as to listen to his honeyed words, to drink in every syllable with secret rapture? He had not once mentioned love, yet she had fallen into his embrace as though he had promised her heaven forever.

She washed and dressed like an automaton, her mind turning over the same ground again and again. Even if he had tired of her, why would he have left her to fend for herself at the lodge? She knew the answer well enough. He had gone after Luis, and he did not want her around when he caught up with him. All his promises had been dust in the face of the wind.

The road back to anything resembling civilisation was a long and arduous track, but she could not simply stay in the lodge and wait for supplies to run out. What choice did she have but to start back towards the Centre and hope that she could make it there before nightfall?

She had been on the road less than fifteen minutes when she heard the sound of a vehicle coming her way, and her heart jolted sharply against her ribcage as she peered into the distance. Disappointment slid around her like a dark cloak minutes later as Carmela pulled up beside her.

'I have been travelling so long,' Carmela said, jumping out of the van. 'I could not believe it when Alejo rang me from his car phone and asked me to pick you up here and take you back to the Centre. What on earth is happening? He has gone to Trevillo, of all places, even though I told him about the quake up there.'

'The quake?' Deanna queried, dredging up her voice from its pit of despair. 'What quake?'

'It happened in the early hours of this morning. It was not too bad, I think, from the reports that have come out over the radio, but there has been some damage. Alejo would not listen to me, though, when I told him. He just cut me off and insisted—insisted, would you know—that I come out here and fetch you.'

'I'm so sorry, Carmela,' Deanna said unhappily. 'I had no idea that you would be put to so much trouble.'

'Trouble?' the other girl said, with a shake of her head. 'It is no trouble, of course. I am happy to help you, but I do not understand what is going on, and Alejo absolutely refused to explain. "I will see you in a day or so, my sweet," he said, "and we will go to the States together and visit your family." That was all. Can you believe it?'

Deanna's stomach tightened convulsively. He had never professed to love her. She had known from the beginning that his relationship with Carmela was more affectionate and loving than anything she might have faintly hoped for. What an incredibly stupid, stupid fool she had been to even entertain the idea that he might feel anything deeply for her.

Dully her glance ran over the contents of the van, loaded up already for its round of deliveries. 'We must go to Trevillo,' she said flatly, and Carmela looked at her as if she had truly and definitely gone mad.

'You are both of you crazy,' she said. 'Why would you want to go to Trevillo?'

'There's someone there I need to find.' It might be too late, but at least she knew where the cottage was situated, and she would be able to head straight for it.

'Alejo said I must on no account take you there,' Carmela said with a deepening frown.

'Then you must tell him,' Deanna said, climbing into the driver's seat and turning the key in the ignition, 'that I hijacked your van. Will you stay here, in the lodge? It may not be safe in Trevillo, but there are enough provisions here for at least a couple of days, and I'll get back to you as quickly as I can.'

'No, no. I will come with you.' Carmela scrambled around to the passenger's side and slid into the seat. 'Now I know you are mad,' she declared, throwing up her hands in mock-horror. 'Or perhaps it is that this person you are going after is very important to you?'

'He is,' Deanna said grimly. 'He is.'

Trevillo was a scene of frantic activity when they arrived there. There was a lot of structural damage, but it seemed that the main focus of devastation had centred on those buildings which were used as offices and were thankfully unoccupied during the night. Deanna's limbs were like lead as she made her way with Carmela to the area where Luis had once lived, and saw people there removing rubble and shattered timber. Her enquiries were fruitless. No one knew anything about Luis San Martin, it seemed. Perhaps he had been here and gone within the space of hours.

She edged her way cautiously along what once had been a street. At the far end, one man stood out among the workers, tall and authoritative, as he directed operations. A stretcher was being carried out from one of the wrecked houses, and she saw a young girl, a teenager perhaps, her face pale, her arm splinted at her side. The men bearing the stretcher paused, as Alejo leaned over and took the girl's free hand in his own, talking to her quietly. The girl's taut frown relaxed a little, and as Alejo pointed out a route through the rubble the men set off once more. Deanna could not prevent the painful lurch of her senses as she watched him turn and begin once more to pull at fallen masonry and the debris of what had once been someone's home.

He looked up as she approached, the dark glitter of his eyes slanting over her in cold disbelief. There was no guilt, no remorse, no vestige of any warm emotion. 'What are you doing here?' he demanded. 'You should be back at the Centre by now.'

'Whatever gave you the idea that I would simply turn around and head for home?' she returned with cool acrimony. 'There are things I have to attend to, as well you know.'

'Your attention would be best placed at the Centre. There is work to be done there.'

'It can wait,' she said tightly.

He threw her an icy, stinging glance, then looked beyond her to Carmela. 'This place is not safe for you, Carmela,' he gritted, moving to hold the girl in his firm grasp. 'You should not have come.'

Deanna fought hard to control the swift flood of jealousy that swept through her as she saw the way he acted with Carmela. How totally different he had been with herself—there had been no trace of welcome for her, had there, no open arms to enfold her? And seeing him wrap himself around her friend was just too much.

She looked away. Why had he made love to her when he felt so much for another woman? Men had a different attitude from women when it came to sex, she knew that, but it made her feel ill to think that he could behave that way. Perhaps he justified it to himself by reasoning that Carmela's feelings towards him were ambivalent, and until such time as she made up her mind one way or the other he might as well make the most of the chances that came his way. He had said himself that his blood ran hot, and he would scarcely be inclined to refuse what was so willingly offered.

Shame coursed through her when she thought of how desperately she had wanted his lovemaking. How eagerly she had fallen into his hands and how quickly he had followed up his advantage and whittled from her the information he had wanted all along.

His voice, a low rumble of angry concern, intruded on her consciousness, and she turned back to see him frowning darkly at Carmela. 'Why did you go against my instructions?' he growled. 'You knew that I did not want you here.'

'For goodness' sake,' Deanna said tersely, 'stop harassing the poor girl. I didn't leave her any choice, if you must know. It's my fault that she's here.'

'Of that I have no doubt,' he said nastily, putting Carmela to one side and coming to menace her with his sheer height. 'It is what I might have expected from you. Not only do you insist on coming here where it is plain you are not wanted, but you drag someone else along with you.'

Guilt racked her as she acknowledged the truth behind his harsh accusation. She'd had no right to bring Carmela out here.

'Alejo, you must not be such a bully,' Carmela said fiercely. 'She is very upset about her friend, as you would be if someone you cared about might be lying hurt in some broken-down building. Treat her gently, please. I will not have you chastise her so.'

His face hardened into a granite mask. 'Chastise?' he hissed. 'That seems such a minor word for what I would like to do to her.'

He glared at her and Deanna glowered back at him. 'The feeling is mutual,' she said, hurt by his scathing contempt.

'Oh, my,' Carmela said in helpless bewilderment. 'I give up trying to understand either of you.'

'Go home, Carmela,' Deanna said. 'I'll find some other transport to take me back—but you could leave some of the supplies. The bandages and other dressings might be needed.'

'I will stay,' the girl announced, and earned herself a lacerating glance from Alejo.

'*Dios!*' he exploded, giving way to a voluble stream of Spanish that made Deanna's ears begin to burn. 'This is insupportable. I am surrounded by females intent on throwing themselves into danger like lemmings. I have no time for this; I have things to do.'

Carmela waited for the blast to die down. 'I shall unload the van,' she said.

'Any people who are hurt and needing treatment are being taken to the schoolhouse,' Alejo told her raspingly. 'It is a solid building, in an area untouched by any movement. Go there, if you must.'

She gave him a sweet smile and walked away.

He turned his simmering rage on Deanna. She had brought his girlfriend into danger and she was going to suffer the cutting lash of his tongue. 'I have never met a more wilful, stubborn, impetuous woman than you,' he said with caustic vehemence. 'Why could you not leave things as they were instead of rushing up here at the first opportunity?'

'You had no right to leave me alone at the lodge. It was a despicable thing to do.'

'You were not alone for more than a couple of hours. I made sure that you would be collected.'

'I didn't want to be collected,' she threw back with mounting fury. 'How dared you leave me behind when you must have known how worried I would be?'

'You would have been informed about what was happening in due course.'

His cool arrogance took her breath away. 'In due course?' she stormed. 'Forget *in due course*. I want to know now, this minute, what has been going on.'

He inclined his head briefly. '*De acuerdo*. Since you are here, I shall do my best to answer your questions... when you are calm.'

'I am perfectly calm.' She dragged air into her lungs. 'How bad is it? Do we have the full picture yet?'

'No one has been killed, we believe, and most of the injured are suffering from fractures, grazes and the like. Of course, many are shocked. A few people are trapped inside these buildings, but we can see them easily enough, and they are conscious. We shall have them out within the hour.'

'Have all these houses been checked?' she asked anxiously, letting her arm sweep in a wide gesture to cover the house where Luis had once lived.

His eyes were dark, his thoughts locked away behind closed shutters as he watched her. 'They have. This was the very first area to be searched by the relief workers.'

'I see.' A slow, aching sigh left her. 'And Luis?' she said, her voice barely above a whisper.

'He was found some hours ago.'

She stared at him, the colour seeping from her face. 'What state was he in? Was he hurt badly?'

'Not by the quake. But he was in no condition to run anywhere. He had a gunshot wound in his leg.'

'Oh, no.' Sickness clawed at her as all her worst fears were confirmed, and she clutched at a crumbling wall for support. Ashen-faced, she stared at Alejo. 'How is he? Is the bullet still in him? Is the wound badly infected?' Her mind ran in turmoil. 'Where is he now?' She looked into the distance towards the schoolhouse, turning as her thoughts gathered speed.

'I hope you are not thinking of going after him,' Alejo said harshly, 'because if you are you would have a long and fruitless journey ahead of you. The bullet is still in place, and he has a slight fever. He has been taken to the hospital. No one will be allowed to see him for some time yet.'

Hospital. That was something at least. 'Then I can go to him.'

'No. It is as I said. No one will see him. He is under armed police guard.'

Her jaw worked with bitter tension. 'I imagine you played a large part in that?'

'I did. I told you that I would deal with the matter, and now it is finished. There is nothing more to be done, and you are not needed here.'

Her heart twisted painfully. It had been exactly as she had imagined. As soon as he had extracted from her the information he needed, he had wasted no time in hunting down Luis, and alerting the police. He felt that he had been wronged, and he had gone relentlessly after the man he believed responsible and brought him to account. She could not condemn him for his actions, but it hurt so badly to know how casually he had used her. And what hurt even more, what was a searing, knife-like thrust through her body, was that she still loved him. No matter what he had done, her love for him remained, locked up in an ice-cold vault of broken dreams.

'You should go now,' he said. 'I have work to do here, and it is work for men alone, with equipment to remove the stonework. Find Carmela, and take her home.'

She turned away, her mind numb, her eyes unseeing. People's lives had been shattered in this place, and in a way she felt that her life too had fragmented, been splintered into a thousand pieces that could never be put back together.

She didn't go to find Carmela. Instead, she picked up a case of dressings that the other girl had thoughtfully left behind, and began to walk along the devastated street.

Passing by one of the buildings, she heard the ominous sound of crumbling brickwork, the sudden gritty rattle of mortar and plasterboard as more of the fabric of the house began to break away. She stopped and looked in through the open doorway, horrified by the torn remains of what was once someone's living-room.

'*Ayudeme, por favor.*'

The voice dragged her attention to a far corner of the room, where a man sat on the bare floor, his back supported by the wall, his legs stretched out in front of him. From the peculiar angle of one of them, it looked as though it was broken.

She hurried to his side. 'Of course I'll help you.'

'Men are bringing a stretcher,' he said, 'but this last fall of material from the ceiling has damaged my wrist, and I have nothing to stop the bleeding.'

'Don't worry, I have something.'

'*Gracias, señorita.*'

She stayed with him, kneeling by his side, until the men arrived with the stretcher, then stood back and watched as they carried him out of the house to the safety of the makeshift medical centre. The sudden crack of plasterboard above her head and the creaking of joists came without warning, too late for her to make it to the door. There was a heavy thud, a stunning blow on the side of her head, and then a slow falling into empty blackness.

Somewhere, in the confusion that followed, she became aware of jumbled voices, urgent mutterings and shouted commands, but each time she tried to make sense of them the black void returned to swallow her up. At one point she registered dazedly that she was being lifted in strong, capable arms, and the faintest whiff of musk assailed her nostrils before she drifted back into those sable depths once more.

The dark spells had no meaning for her at all, they were mere blanks in the passage of time, but the bouts of sickness that claimed her in between them left her feeling wretched and drained of all strength.

Someone was gently wiping her face with a damp cloth, and a soothingly deep voice said, 'You will soon feel better, Deanna. The doctor will give you an injection, just a slight sting, and then perhaps you will be able to sleep.'

The cool, restful voice floated around her, and she put her trust in it, accepting the quiet promise it held out to her. The ache in her head subsided a little, and she sank back into peaceful, uncomplicated slumber.

When she woke, finally, what must have been aeons later, she blinked her eyes and stared around at the unfamiliar shadows in the darkened room. She was surrounded by softness—a downy quilt, plump pillows, a mattress that seemed to flow around her.

'So you are awake at last.' Alejo moved into the pale glow cast by a solitary lamp, and frowned down at her. 'How are you feeling?'

She stared at his tall, dark shape, outlined in the golden light. 'I don't know what happened,' she said in confusion. 'Is this your home? I don't remember how I came here.' She struggled to sit up.

'Yes, you are in my house,' he told her. 'Lie still.' His hand curved around her shoulder, easing her backwards. 'You were knocked out by a wooden beam, but the doctor thinks there has been no lasting damage. Two blows on the head in a few short days is enough for anyone, I think.'

Her brows edged together. 'It's all very hazy. I remember being in a house and there was a man being carried out, but the rest is a bit of a blank.'

'It is nothing to worry about. You were concussed for a time, and you kept passing out.'

Vague memories stirred. 'I was sick,' she said flatly.

'Very.' His mouth made a wry twist, and she sank back against the pillows, feeling the slow burn of mortification creep through her body. Was there to be no end to the humiliating displays she made of herself in front of this man? It was bad enough to have been thrown to one side like an unwrapped parcel whose contents no longer held any interest for him, but to have been sick in front of him—that was surely reaching rock-bottom.

She ran her tongue over the dryness of her lips, and he said consideringly, 'Are you thirsty?'

'Yes, I am.'

From a jug on the bedside table, he poured out a long, iced fruit drink and handed it to her. 'Here you are, then. Drink up and I'll get you a refill.'

The brush of his fingers against her bare arm brought tingling vitality to her skin. She glanced up at him quickly, but if the brief contact had any effect on him it did not register in his expression. She was wearing a silk nightdress, not one of her own, and she wondered to whom it belonged, and, more feverishly, who had put it on her.

Taking a long swallow of the juice, she savoured the cool liquid as it slid down her throat. Holding out the empty glass to him when she had finished, she was careful to avoid his touch.

'Thank you,' she said quietly, subdued. 'Who lent me the nightdress? I'd like to thank whoever it was.'

'No thanks are necessary,' he said smoothly. 'It is new, a gift for you. I believe I estimated the size correctly, didn't I?'

She hated the betraying heat that swept along her cheekbones. 'I—yes, thank you.' Hesitantly, she asked him, 'Who helped me to dress?'

His mouth curved. 'I think your question really is who helped you to *undress*?' His gleaming gaze danced over her. 'How can you possibly still be embarrassed after the night we spent together? There is not one part of you I have not seen, Deanna. Don't you think your modesty is a trifle out of place?'

Her insides curled in an agony of remembrance. How could he talk about it so easily, without any qualm or hint of reticence? No doubt the whole episode, as far as he was concerned, could be dismissed as something casual, which was simply a normal part of his everyday life. It was galling to be confronted by such blatant unconcern. It might well be commonplace to him, she thought with sharp, uncomfortable resentment, but she was not used to being naked in front of any man.

'Enough, Deanna,' he said in amusement. 'You need not squirm so. If it will put your mind at rest, you must know that it was my housekeeper who saw to your more intimate needs.'

Relief washed over her. 'I'm glad of that. I must thank you for taking care of me, for bringing me here. You didn't have to do that...I could have gone to the hospital, perhaps—although I suppose they were overloaded with emergency cases...' Her voice trailed off on a troubled note.

'I would not hear of it,' he said with cold severity, haughty arrogance moulding his features. 'You are my responsibility.'

Her fingers clamped jerkily on the coverlet. Of course, in a way, she supposed, he was in the nature of an employer, since it was his money that helped to fund the Centre. Perhaps that made him feel honour-bound to do something about her. He need not feel that way for long, she decided. Just as soon as she was strong enough, she would get up and leave. In fact, now was as good a time as any. Pushing back the quilt, she swung her legs over the side of the bed.

'What do you think you are doing now?' Exasperation threaded his voice.

She stared up at him groggily, a wave of faintness making her head swim. 'I thought I would get up,' she muttered, feeling cautiously along the edge of the bed for support.

'You will do no such thing,' he said restrictively, tugging on the bell-pull at the side of the bed. 'You will stay there until you are fully recovered.' With a firm hand, he settled her back in the bed, and for the moment she was too overcome by dizziness to put up any kind of a fight.

'Is there any news of Luis?' she asked, once the room had stopped spinning.

His mouth tightened. 'He is improving slowly. The bullet has been removed.'

'Thank goodness. Has there been any sign of the men that were following him?'

'You should not be troubling yourself with these things. It is all being dealt with.'

What kind of answer was that? At least, though, he was safe for the moment.

'I think it would be best if you try to eat something,' he said. 'I have asked Rosana to bring a tray for you.'

'I'm not hungry.'

He sat down on the edge of the bed and lifted her hand in his. 'Please don't argue with me, Deanna. I don't like living in a constant battlefield, and it would please me immensely if you will try just a morsel, to build up your strength.'

There was a knock on the door, and Rosana came in with the promised laden tray. 'I have brought you some home-made soup,' she said. 'It is light and nourishing, and I'm sure if you can manage it you will soon be feeling a little better.'

'Thank you, Rosana.' With both of them staring at her, willing her to eat, what could she do? She picked up her spoon and tasted it. 'It's delicious,' she murmured.

Satisfied, Rosana left them alone, and Deanna made some inroads on the meal before pushing it away, and daring Alejo's frown of displeasure.

'You look tired,' he said. 'It is probably time for you to rest again. Shall I help you to the bathroom first?'

His polite consideration was unnerving when what she really, desperately wanted was to be taken into his arms and kissed soundly. The futile thought withered as fast as it had come, and she settled instead for the supporting strength of his arm as he led her to the bathroom.

'How does your head feel now?' he asked as he helped her back into the bed and arranged the covers around her.

'It's much better,' she said. 'Just aching and a little sore—I shall be out of here before you know it.'

'I should imagine it is a great deal sore,' he commented drily, handing her two tablets and a glass of juice. 'The doctor has left these pain-killers. Take them, they will help.' He waited while she followed his bidding, then went on, 'He will call again to see you in the morning—by then you will probably be feeling much more like your normal self, heaven help us all.'

She sent him a sharp glance, catching the dart of amusement that flickered in his eyes. 'I shall be well enough to go back to my flat,' she vowed firmly.

'There is no rush for you to leave my house,' he told her sharply. 'I shall not be here in the morning, I have a plane to catch, but my housekeeper has strict instructions as to your welfare. You will not allow her to risk my disapproval by trying to persuade her to go against them.'

He was going away. His words hit her full-on, worse than any blow she had encountered so far. Suddenly she felt sick again, her stomach heaving convulsively, and she bent her head to hide her shattering disappointment from him. Of course he was going. What had she expected?

'Carmela told me you were taking her to the States,' she said huskily when she had herself under control.

'That's right.' He looked at her quickly and she averted her gaze once more. 'She is going to see her family. It will be a prolonged visit, so that she can see her mother through her operation, and watch her recovery. You needn't worry about the workload at the Centre, though. Arrangements have been made for someone to cover for her—you do not mind this?'

'No... no.' She cleared her throat. 'That's quite all right. I know she's worried about her mother.'

He reached for her, tucking his fingers beneath her chin and tilting her head so that he could look into her face. 'You are pale again. I have tired you.' He pressed her gently back against the pillows, then placed his palm lightly on her forehead, checking her temperature. 'Close your eyes,' he commanded. 'Go to sleep and let the tablets do their work.'

She did as she was told, swamped by a dispiriting wash of weariness. Perhaps if she slept long enough she would wake up one day and find that this well of misery had drained itself dry.

He let himself out of the room quietly, and as the door closed behind him and she heard his firm tread moving along the passageway the tears that were banked behind her eyes seeped through the dam and fell silently down her cheeks.

CHAPTER NINE

As SOON as the doctor had pronounced her on the road to recovery the next morning, Deanna insisted on returning to her own flat at the Centre, much to Rosana's dismay.

'Señor de Rocas expected you to stay for much longer than this,' she said unhappily. 'He is very concerned about your welfare, and he said you were on no account to go anywhere until that bump on the back of your head had disappeared and there were no more after-effects.'

'I'm feeling fine now,' Deanna stressed firmly. 'He believes he has some responsibility for me, but that isn't true, Rosana. I'm quite capable of taking care of myself, and besides, I have to get back to the Centre to see Junket. She'll pine if I'm away too long. Apart from which, with Carmela going away, I have to organise the workload for her temporary replacement.'

Rosana shook her head, her eyes troubled. 'I am sure he did not intend you to go back to work so soon. He will be very angry with me.'

'Not with you, Rosana,' Deanna assured her grimly. 'If he's going to blame anyone, it will be me, and he can hardly tear a strip off me if he's in the States, now can he?'

None of her arguments would remove the anxious frown from Rosana's face, but she had to concede defeat in the end and allow Deanna to go her own way.

Once she was back at the Centre, Deanna tried to put her all energy into her work, but it was hard to concentrate when her mind kept wandering in wearying, lonely circles, and everything she did seemed like an uphill climb. Knowing that he was with Carmela plunged her into the black depths of despair, and the nausea which plagued her every time she thought of the two of them wrapped up in each other's arms was far worse than anything she had experienced before.

Pinning a fresh schedule to the noticeboard two days later, she reflected miserably that in coming to Peru her whole life had changed. She had loved, and lost, and the pain would stay with her through all the empty years that stretched ahead. Even her attempts to help Luis had been disastrous. They would not even let her speak to him by phone, and she had no idea what was going on.

The sound of gravel being thrown up on the drive outside dragged her reluctant attention back to the office and the work which was still to be done. Could this be Carmela's replacement already? She wasn't due here until next week.

The door slammed back on its hinges, and the smile she had tried to summon up in greeting froze on her face as Alejo strode towards her, his long, lean body almost vibrating with anger.

'What is the meaning of this?' he demanded harshly, his words stabbing at her like so many stingingly sharp knives.

Her mouth dropped open, shock holding her rigid for several moments and his impatience at her bleak silence grew like a thundercloud gathering momentum before the storm.

'I asked you a question,' he said, his teeth clamped together with barely contained fury. 'You will answer me.'

Her voice came out as a hoarse whisper. 'I thought you were in the States.'

'And as soon as my back is turned you seize your chance to rush back here and go against all that I have said. Did you imagine that I would not check on you? Didn't I tell you that I am kept informed of everything that goes on in my own household?'

'Is—is that why you've come back so soon?' she faltered. 'Has something happened at the plantation, or——' a sudden, terrible thought struck her '—or is it something to do with Luis?'

A muscle flicked in a tight spasm along the line of his jaw. 'I see,' he growled, 'that you are still eaten up with your abiding obsession for this man and all that concerns him. You would be wise to clear him from your mind, once and for all.'

Her face paled. 'I don't understand,' she said shakily. 'What has happened? Please tell me. No one will tell me anything. They won't even let me talk to him——'

'You have tried to make contact with him?' His tone was brittle.

She spread her hands in a helpless gesture. 'Do you think that I can just switch off, pretend that everything is rosy, when my friend is a prisoner, waiting to be thrown into gaol as soon as he's regained his strength? I know that this is what you wanted, that you've achieved all you set out to do, but you can hardly expect me to be beside myself with joy.'

The shock of seeing him again was doing alarming things to her nervous system, and she swayed slightly, steadying herself against the hard surface of a cupboard.

The diamond glitter flared once more in his eyes, his glance raked her white face. 'You are still not well,' he said. 'You should not be here.'

'There's nothing wrong with me,' she corrected him. 'I've just been a little anxious, that's all.'

'You have lost weight,' he accused, running a disapproving glance over her silk wrap-over dress. 'Why have you not been eating?'

Because the mere thought of food made my stomach churn, she recalled silently. Because you took me to the heights, then threw me down and, even knowing that you don't want me, I can't help but love you.

Aloud, she said dismissively, 'My appetite is coming back gradually.' At least he was here, and showing signs of concern. Perhaps he would talk to her, tell her what was happening to Luis. That was all she could hope for. 'Would you like coffee?' she asked.

He said brusquely, 'I did not come here for coffee and polite drawing-room conversation. You are much too tense for your own good. Sit down, before you fall down.' He indicated the small office couch.

Stiffly, she did as he asked. 'I want to know about Luis,' she said stiltedly, 'about what is happening to him.'

He studied her taut features, then sat down beside her and said, 'It seems that this man colours your every waking thought. And you believe that my dislike for him runs so deep that I would do anything to see him put away for a long time, am I right?' Her fingers worked destructively in the fine silk of her dress and his hands came down on hers, stilling them. 'Am I right?' he persisted.

'What else am I to think?' she returned uneasily, her pulses beginning to throb in frantic yearning at his casually warm possession of her hands. 'Since the first moment we met, your one goal has been to track him down and see him destroyed.'

'Not quite.' His fingers slid caressingly over her soft skin. 'My first thoughts were of righting a wrong, of seeking the man who was responsible for cheating me, and making him account for his actions. It was only after I began to know you that I wanted him out of the picture, removed from your life forever.'

She stared up at him, aghast, her blue eyes filled with pain. 'But why? That's insane,' she whispered. 'I don't understand.'

His mouth made a rueful slant. 'Perhaps I was crazy for a while. I wanted you so badly, I could think of nothing but you. You filled my every waking thought, my dreams even. When I thought of you and him together, I could have killed him.'

He had wanted her. She had known from the beginning that desire blazed fiercely beneath the barely civilised exterior, but it was a desire that had burned itself out in one wild and searing conflagration.

A cold shiver racked her body, and he ran his hands up over her arms, moulding the fragile bones of her shoulders beneath his fingers. 'But I managed—just—to control my feelings of violence towards this man,' he muttered. 'You cared for him, you believed in his innocence... and you had not slept with him.' His eyes darkened. 'I had hope, when you gave yourself to me so willingly, *querida*, just a small flickering ray of light at the end of the dark passageway.'

She looked at him guardedly, trying to quell the faint leap of her heart, bewilderment reflected in her eyes. He spoke of hope, as though he might have wanted their relationship to continue—yet he had left her the very next morning, with cold, frightening deliberation. His smile held a tinge of bitter irony. 'But it is news of your friend that occupies your thoughts. You will not rest until you have been to see him, so perhaps that is what we had better do.' He stood up abruptly, pulling her with him. 'He is no longer in the hospital, but has been taken to a place near to my home to finish his recuperation. Come, I will take you there.'

This sudden turn of events took her breath away, and she travelled with him in a dream-like state, the Range Rover covering the miles with ease. Alejo spoke very little to her on the journey, fixing his concentration on the winding road to the plantation, but Deanna's troubled mind would not settle.

'Is he still under armed guard?' she asked.

'No. It was no longer thought to be necessary.'

She stared at him. 'But—if he's recovering, won't he be more likely to try to escape?' She faltered, puzzled and uncertain.

'The guard was never there as a restriction. He was not under arrest. Is that what you thought?' He shook his head. 'It was for his own safety.'

She gazed at him in stunned confusion and he added, 'Your friend is quite safe, Deanna. He will not be going to gaol.'

His words sent a ray of hope to shimmer through her body. 'You mean...you're not pressing charges against him?'

'How could I, when he has done nothing wrong? I am not so blinded by my own prejudices that I would not seek out the truth. In fact, San Martin has done me and the police a great service. He discovered a group of men whose main source of wealth came from making copies of documents and artefacts, the real items being later smuggled out of the country. They had tried to make copies of my own collection, and by tracking down the men responsible San Martin put his own life at risk. It is thanks to your friend that these men are now under lock and key, and my property has been restored to me.'

Deanna's eyes widened, and he gave her a brief smile. 'But he will tell you these things himself.' The Range Rover drew to a halt, and she saw that they had arrived at a small cottage bordering the plantation.

The door was opened by a matronly woman dressed in the neat uniform of a nurse.

'Come in,' she said, recognising Alejo, and standing to one side. 'The patient is feeling much better, if his irascible mood is anything to go by. I think he is beginning to find the restrictions of his healing leg frustrating.'

She showed them into a sitting-room, furnished simply with two easy-chairs and a glass-fronted cabinet at one end, and a shelving unit full of plants taking up most of one wall. A long, low settee occupied the central space, and there Luis sat, his injured leg supported by several plump cushions. He turned as they walked in.

'Deanna!' he exclaimed, and she ran to him, clasping her arms about him as he hugged her close. 'I am so happy to see you, Deanna,' he said.

'And I'm overjoyed to see you,' Deanna told him, brushing the dampness from her eyes as she gazed at him. 'You can't know how worried I've been. I tried so hard to get to you in time, and I was so unhappy when I reached the lodge and you had gone. You must have been in danger the whole time, and I felt so useless, knowing that you were hurt.'

'All is well now, as you can see, thanks to Señor de Rocas. He has hired a nurse to take care of me. She is an ogress, and I will tell you secretly I am terrified of her.' He looked across at Alejo, who said nothing, but regarded their entwined bodies in taut silence.

Deanna straightened. 'Please tell me what happened,' she urged him. 'You have no excuse now.'

'You have probably guessed most of it,' Luis said. 'I took two pots to an expert for valuation, and collected them from him a couple of days later. When I arrived home with them, I discovered that I was in possession of fakes. It would not have been easy for anyone to detect, but I knew of a tiny flaw in one of the gems, and this alerted me to the fact that the vessels had been switched at some point on my journey.'

His expression was grim. 'Someone must have gained access to the valuer's premises in order to make copies, and I made it my business to track down those who had done this thing. I did not know then what I was dealing with, how ruthless they could be. When I threatened them with police action, they laughed in my face. Then they turned their guns on me. They did not shoot, at that time, but it was a narrow escape, I think. What proof did I have? they asked. The real pots were on their way to be smuggled out of the country, yet I was the one who had removed them from their rightful owner, and obtained a valuation on them. It was my word against theirs. They were respected men in the community, and I was the one who was to take the blame.'

He glanced at Alejo, before turning back to Deanna. 'Señor de Rocas has told you of the note that was shown to him. It implicated me in this business, insinuating that I had instigated the forgeries, but I would never have done that. How could I prove my innocence, though? They said they would kill me if I went back to the plantation, or if I spoke to Señor de Rocas or the police. I believed them. There is much money involved in these things, and when they said they would make sure that I had left town I had no doubt that they meant it.'

'That must have been the day of the fiesta,' Deanna said. 'That was when you were afraid you were being followed.'

'That's right. Even so, I could not let matters rest there. I felt responsible for Señor de Rocas's loss, and I had decided that I would try to find out where the pots had been sent for transportation.'

'And when you found them you sent them to me,' Deanna supplied.

'I could not be sure that any parcel going to the plantation would not be intercepted. They did not know you, and so you were safe.'

'But you were wounded—how did that happen?'

His mouth made a rueful twist. 'I was careless. I was seen removing the package, and if I hadn't managed to throw myself on the back of a moving vehicle I think that would have been the end of me. As it was, I escaped long enough to give them a runaround. I knew that they would come after me— by this time I was fairly sure of names and places, and they feared that they would be convicted for sure, on my evidence. I took refuge for a few hours with a friend, who lives in an isolated cabin in the hills. He promised to send the parcel to you, and he said that he would notify the police. I dared not stay with him. I did not know how close they were, and my friend lent me one of his trucks so that I could get away.'

'And the lodge?'

'I am so sorry about that.' A deep line etched its way into his forehead. 'I truly thought I had lost them when I reached that place, otherwise I would never have asked for your help. As it turned out, I was wrong, and I had to give them the slip once more and make my way to Trevillo. You know the rest.'

Deanna gave a shuddery sigh. 'Thank heaven you're safe now.'

He grasped her hands drawing her to him. 'I am sorry if I brought you anxiety, Deanna. I did not mean to give you heartache—when I heard that you had been hurt in Trevillo——'

Alejo stepped forward. 'She is well enough now that she is in my care. You can relinquish her to me.' It was a veiled command, his dark eyes narrowed on their clasped fingers, and Luis looked first at him, and then across at Deanna.

'Ah. I see.' A glimmer of amusement started in his eyes and Deanna fidgeted restlessly.

'I don't think you do,' she muttered. He was putting the wrong interpretation on things. She was certain, from that purely male gleam, that he had totally the wrong idea. He did not know about Carmela, about the way Alejo had left her at the lodge.

'You look pale,' Luis told her. 'Go with Señor de Rocas. I am glad you are in good hands.'

'We shall go to my home,' Alejo said. 'I have things to attend to.'

There was nothing hidden in Alejo's determination to leave. It was as he said, they had been there long enough, and he had work to do.

She stood up slowly, and planted a brief kiss on Luis's cheek. 'I'm so relieved that you're getting your strength back. Please don't do anything like that again. My nerves won't stand it.'

He laughed. 'I won't, I promise. From now on I am the soul of conservative behaviour.'

Alejo led her out to the Range Rover, and she sank back in the upholstered seat with a long sigh of relief. 'I knew he had done nothing wrong. Oh, I'm so glad that everything has turned out all right in the end. I couldn't have borne it if he'd been thrown into gaol. Thank you for listening to him and for helping him with his recovery. It was wonderful of you to do that.'

'It was necessary.'

His mouth was set in a taut line as he drove towards the plantation, and she realised that his business must be preoccupying him. That was why he was so silent and withdrawn. Or was it that he was missing Carmela? Had she decided against him? Was that the reason for his speedy return from the States?

They had arrived at the house, and he showed her into the large, exquisitely furnished lounge.

'I will fix some drinks,' he said. 'What would you prefer? Coffee, fruit juice, or something stronger?'

'Juice will be fine, thank you.' She went over to the wide couch and sat down, and in a few moments he was by her side, handing her a glass.

'Thank you for taking me to see him,' she murmured, tracing a frosted line around the sparkling crystal with the tip of her finger.

'Has it put your mind at ease?'

She looked at him, her mouth softening with pleasure. 'Oh, yes. You must know it has.'

'I am glad to hear it.' He drained the amber liquid in his glass in one long swallow, and she watched the movements of his bronzed throat in wide-eyed fascination. 'It is to be hoped that your appetite will improve by leaps and bounds from this moment.'

'What will happen now?'

His brow rose. 'In what respect?'

He placed his glass on the table with a faint snap, and she said quickly, 'I mean about his work. Will he be able to finish cataloguing your collection now?' She was startled to see the dark tension groove his face, the repressed anger tightening his mouth.

'I dare say he will continue working on it in due course, and then move on to other commissions. I have friends who need this service and will be pleased to act on my recommendation.'

'But that's wonderful.' She studied him, puzzled by the scarcely hidden antagonism she sensed in his manner. 'You're being very generous.'

'It is the least I can do. Besides, it is not done without some self-interest.' His glance narrowed on her face, his dark eyes intent. 'My friends will live some distance away, a matter of several days' journeying. You will not find it so easy to make contact with him, you understand?'

She stared at him oddly, a strange tension building in her, and he said tersely, 'I said earlier that I had my feelings under control, but they are not so much in control that I can stand by and see you with San Martin.'

Head bent, she slid her tumbler on to the table and smoothed down the silk of her dress. 'Why should that bother you so much? Has Carmela turned you down? Is that why you came back here so quickly?'

'What is this talk of Carmela?' His voice rumbled around her, a vein of astonishment running through it. 'She is where she wants to be, with her family, and José.'

Her glance shot to his face. 'José is with her?'

'Of course,' he said with impatience. 'I arranged it as soon as we arrived in the States. He will keep her company and bring her back when she is ready to leave. They are two people made for each other. Surely you knew that? She is very jealous of him, but he would never so much as look at another woman. I cannot understand what has been going through your head.' He studied her flushed face with sparking curiosity, a faint gleam coming to life in the depths of his dark eyes. 'You thought that she and I had gone away to be together?' His mouth curved, all at once attractive and infinitely dangerous to her peace of mind.

'What else would I have thought?' she said with some diffidence, turning away from his piercingly sharp gaze. 'You're always sliding your arms around each other; you made no secret of the way you felt.'

'This has bothered you, Deanna *mia*?' She did not answer and he wound his arms around her, pulling her to him. 'Then I have much to hope for, after all. It seems I was not wrong in thinking your response to me that night at the lodge was founded of more than just a seeking for comfort and the need to discover for yourself this new experience. There was more to it than that, wasn't there, *querida*, much more?'

'Why should you believe that?' she muttered, struggling in a futile effort to free herself from the binding circle of his arms. 'It meant nothing whatever to you, only a quick conquest, a way of making the hours pass more agreeably.'

His hold on her tightened. 'How can you say this to me? Do you think I make a habit of such things? You are very wrong, *enamorada*, very wrong indeed.'

'I wish,' she said desperately, fighting a losing battle against her longing to succumb to the sweet lure of his embrace, 'that you would let me go. I'm not here to satisfy your momentary whims. Leave me alone, Alejo. Go and find someone else to cater to your sensual appetite.'

'You are asking the impossible,' he protested huskily. 'It is not a momentary thing I feel for you. I have wanted no one else since the moment we met; the need for you has been like a fire raging in my blood, and nothing can assuage it.' His lips brushed the sensitive line of her throat, meandered across the softness of her cheek. 'I want you, Deanna; why do you keep me in such torment?'

'I don't believe you're suffering at all,' she muttered thickly. 'Your need for me will last no longer than the time it takes to get me into bed, and after that I'll be lucky to see the back of your heels in the distance.'

'You pierce me to the heart with such talk,' he said roughly. 'How can you believe this?'

'It's easy enough. I only have to think back to the way you left me so abruptly, so coldly, after that one night.' She swallowed against the painful tightness in her throat. 'I meant so much to you that you stole away from me without a backward glance before it was even light.'

'That isn't true, Deanna. I thought long and hard about leaving you that way, but if I had woken you, you would have insisted on coming with me, and it was too dangerous for you in Trevillo. I knew that, of all places, that village might be at risk. There have been tremors there before, and that is why only a few people still choose to live and work there.' His hands smoothed over her, gliding along the fine indentations of her spine, his lips warm against her throat. 'I wanted to leave you where you were safe and secure. I might have known you would find some way of coming after me—I should have sent a man to do the job of taking you back to the Centre, instead of leaving it to a slip of a girl. As it was, look at the way you were hurt. I will never forgive myself for that.'

'But you were so angry with me,' Deanna whispered, her skin burning beneath the lingering pressure of his mouth.

'I did not see any way of getting you out of there, short of driving you myself, and I was needed—there were injured people to be cared for, and I was torn in two by your presence. When you walked away, I could not immediately go after you, and when my first chance came I was too late, you had been knocked down by that beam. When I saw you lying there, crumpled on the ground, I thought the worst, and I felt as though I was bleeding too, as though my life's blood was seeping away. I love you, Deanna. I cannot bear to live without you.'

'You... love me?' Her fingers crept up to touch his face, to trace the wonderful, familiar lines. 'I thought—I never dreamed——' Her heart swelled with joy as she looked at him. 'Oh, hold me, Alejo,' she said in fervent appeal, 'hold me tight, and please, please kiss me.'

He responded with gratifying speed, his mouth moving in fierce possession on hers, his hands urging her to him as though he would be one with her, regardless of the taut restriction of their clothes.

She clung to him, kissing him back with mindless passion, wanting the feel of his hands on her body, driven by a need greater than anything she had known before. Her fingers tangled with the buttons of his shirt, tugging the thin material aside so that she could slide her hands over the beautifully moulded contours of his chest. With wondering eagerness, her lips trailed over his velvety skin, her tongue gliding around his taut male nipples with unashamed, reckless delight.

He groaned his satisfaction against her cheek, his mouth brushing the errant tendrils of hair that feathered around her temples. 'This is not the place,' he said, and she knew a swift flood of disappointment. 'Do not look so sad, *querida*. It is only that I do not wish Rosana to disturb us as she did once before. We shall go upstairs and lock ourselves away from the world.'

She didn't recall taking the stairs. Her feet moved on filmy clouds, she floated, his arm at her waist, supporting her as he drifted kisses over her cheeks and throat. When they reached his room, he shut the door firmly and took her over to the wide, welcoming bed. Her arms wound their way around his neck, drawing him to her, her fingers smoothing over the fine material of his shirt.

Searing her lips with the burning stroke of his mouth, he shrugged his shirt to the floor, her silk dress melting away beneath the impatient glide of his fingers, her underwear joining the small pile gathering on the floor. 'I have never, in my lifetime, wanted anyone so much as I want you,' he said unevenly, moving her back against the pillows and lowering himself over her so that his chest grazed the tight, waiting buds of her breasts. She stretched sinuously, arching to meet him, and he growled hungrily, deep in his throat, savouring the moment, before his mouth swept down to taste the creamy swell and linger on those rosebud crescents.

She was aching with want of him, moving in restless, sinuous abandon beneath him, her hands brushing the rigid evidence of his arousal. He shuddered against her, persuading her of his joy in her sweet possession of his manhood, until the hot pulse of desire became almost too much, and he shifted, his hands shaping her, firming over her supple curves, sliding to tease the sensitised skin of her inner thighs. His touch was a delicious torment, a sweet rapture, and when he found her warm, moist core the fire within her grew to incandescence, threatening to consume her in its leaping flames. He kissed away the cries that broke on her lips, entering her with heated urgency, the rhythmic thrusts of his lovemaking taking her with him to heights she had never dreamed of, a plateau of endless joy, and on, to a volcanic peak of swirling mists and explosive heat. The tension shattered within her, ripples spreading in a widening arc, and then she heard his own muffled shout of exhilaration, felt the tightening band of his arms around her.

'I will never let you go,' he muttered, his voice rough-edged, his breathing laboured. 'You will be mine for all time. Say you will be my wife, *querida*. Say it for me, please.'

'I will, Alejo. I love you so much.' Her fingers curled against his chest, delighting in the supple feel of his smooth flesh. 'But I never dreamed that you would love me in return. When you went away with Carmela, I was so unhappy, I thought my world had come to an end.'

'I did not feel that I had much choice. There were things that the surgeon wished to talk over with me, and I had promised Carmela that I would take her to the States in time for her mother's operation. She puts on a show of being brave and cool, but inside she was afraid, alarmed by the thought of the flight, worried that things might go wrong with the operation, and I knew that she needed my comfort on the journey. I had promised her this—her mother too—but it made you so sad, and I am deeply sorry for that.'

He kissed her tenderly, and when she surfaced once more she said huskily, 'It doesn't matter any more. I thought that you were leaving me forever, and I didn't know how to cope with that. You gave me no sign that you still wanted me...you didn't even kiss me.'

He stroked her hair, winding the springy curls around his fingers. 'You had been so cool with me in Trevillo and there had been no time for explanations between us. Then you were unconscious for a while, and you looked so ill. I dared not touch you, because my passion for you would have been too great. I did not think I could have stopped at a mere kiss, when I wanted to take you in my arms and crush you to me.'

'I didn't know,' she whispered. 'I'm only glad that you came back to me so soon.'

'If you had not been on the road to recovery, I should not have gone, promises or not. But I knew that the danger time was over, and that I was leaving you in safe hands. Even so, you managed to slip away from me.' His fingers stroked the length of her jaw with tender care. 'Our marriage will take place as soon as possible, and from now on you will be firmly installed in my house. I shall have you by my side for always.'

She smiled, snuggling up against the warmth of his chest, soothed by the steady rise and fall of his breathing. 'Aren't you forgetting just a little something?' she asked softly.

His arm curved around her more securely. 'What is that?'

'My work at the Centre. I do rather enjoy it, you know, and I don't think I should like to give it up just yet. Besides, there is Junket to consider.' She pressed her lips to him, revelling in the taste of his male skin.

The rhythm of his breathing altered, his hands clasped her more tightly. 'If you insist,' he said with due consideration, 'then perhaps we shall work out a compromise. You shall work there for a few hours a week. The rest of the time I shall have you to myself.'

In his opinion, he was being gloriously magnanimous, and she smiled again, planting a kiss on his ribcage and sliding her hand over the beautiful perfection of his muscles. 'And Junket?' she queried lightly.

'She belongs with you, and, like you, she is adorable. I shall adopt her.' He threw her a searing look. 'Have I satisfied all your conditions now? You drive a hard bargain, *querida*, and I have it in mind to make you pay. I shall demand from you the sweet promise of a thousand kisses and the soft caress of your warm body next to mine.'

She sighed, moving against him in delicious anticipation. 'Is that what you call payment? she asked huskily. 'When do I start?'

He smiled down at her. 'Right now seems as good a time as any.' Pressuring her back against the pillows, he leaned over her, brushing his lips across the eager softness of her mouth. 'Of course, you may add to your debt as much as you wish as time goes on.' His hands traced the line of her body with warm, possessive urgency. 'Your credit rating is infinite, and we have all the time in the world to explore the possibilities.'

She wound her arms around him. 'I have a feeling,' she murmured happily, 'that these possibilities are going to be endless.'

NEW from...

MILLS & BOON

HEARTS OF FIRE
by Miranda Lee

Welcome to a new and totally compelling family saga set in the glamorous world of opal dealing in Australia.

Laden with dark secrets, forbidden desires and scandalous discoveries. HEARTS OF FIRE unfolds over a series of 6 books as beautiful, innocent Gemma Smith goes in search of a new life, and fate introduces her to Nathan Whitmore, the ruthless, talented and utterly controlled playwright, and acting head of Whitmore Opals.

BUY ONE GET ONE FREE!
As a special introductory offer you can buy
Book 1 - 'Seduction & Sacrifice'
along with
Book 2 - 'Desire & Deception'
for just £2.50

Available from April 1994
Price: £2.50

Available from W. H. Smith, John Menzies, Volume One, Forbuoys, Martins, Woolworths, Tesco, Asda, Safeway and other paperback stockists. Also available from Mills & Boon Reader Service, FREEPOST, PO Box 236, Croydon, Surrey CR9 9EL. (UK Postage & Packing free)

IT'S NEVER TOO LATE FOR SWEET REVENGE...

Adrienne's glittering lifestyle was the perfect foil for her extraordinary talents. A modern princess, flitting from one exclusive gathering to another, no one knew her as The Shadow—the most notorious jewel thief of the decade.

Her spectacular plan to carry out the ultimate heist would even an old and bitter score. But she would need all her stealth and cunning to pull it off —Philip Chamberlain, Interpol's toughest cop knew all the moves and was catching up with her. His only mistake was to fall under Adrienne's seductive spell!

WORLDWIDE

AVAILABLE NOW   PRICE £3.50

Available from W.H. Smith, John Menzies, Martins, Forbuoys, most supermarkets and other paperback stockists. Also available from Worldwide Reader Service, Freepost, PO Box 236, Thornton Road, Croydon, Surrey CR9 9EL. (UK Postage & Packing free)

RELENTLESS AMBITIONS, SHOCKING SECRETS AND POWERFUL DESIRES

Penny Jordan's stunning new novel is not to be missed!

The dramatic story of six very different people—irrevocably linked by ambition and desire, each must face private demons in a riveting struggle for power. Together they must find the strength to emerge from the lingering shadows of the past, into the dawning promise of the future.

WORLDWIDE

AVAILABLE NOW   PRICED AT £4.99

Available from WH Smith, John Menzies, Volume One, Forbuoys, Martins, Woolworths, Tesco, Asda, Safeway and other paperback stockists. Also available from Worldwide Reader Service, FREEPOST, PO Box 236, Croydon, Surrey CR9 9EL. (UK Postage & Packing free)

MILLS & BOON

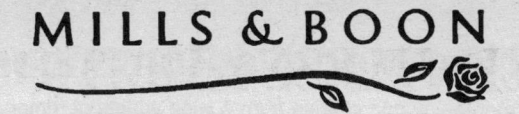

Forthcoming Titles

DUET
Available in April

The Betty Neels Duet A SUITABLE MATCH
THE MOST MARVELLOUS SUMMER

The Emma Darcy Duet PATTERN OF DECEIT
BRIDE OF DIAMONDS

FAVOURITES
Available in April

NOT WITHOUT LOVE Roberta Leigh
NIGHT OF ERROR Kay Thorpe

LOVE ON CALL
Available in April

VET IN A QUANDARY Mary Bowring
NO SHADOW OF DOUBT Abigail Gordon
PRIORITY CARE Mary Hawkins
TO LOVE AGAIN Laura MacDonald

Available from W.H. Smith, John Menzies, Volume One, Forbuoys, Martins, Tesco, Asda, Safeway and other paperback stockists.

Also available from Mills & Boon Reader Service, Freepost, P.O. Box 236, Croydon, Surrey CR9 9EL.

Readers in South Africa - write to:
Book Services International Ltd, P.O. Box 41654, Craighall, Transvaal 2024.

Next Month's Romances

Each month you can choose from a wide variety of romance with Mills & Boon. Below are the new titles to look out for next month, why not ask either Mills & Boon Reader Service or your Newsagent to reserve you a copy of the titles you want to buy – just tick the titles you would like and either post to Reader Service or take it to any Newsagent and ask them to order your books.

Please save me the following titles: Please tick | ✓

Title	Author	
AN UNSUITABLE WIFE	Lindsay Armstrong	
A VENGEFUL PASSION	Lynne Graham	
FRENCH LEAVE	Penny Jordan	
PASSIONATE SCANDAL	Michelle Reid	
LOVE'S PRISONER	Elizabeth Oldfield	
NO PROMISE OF LOVE	Lilian Peake	
DARK MIRROR	Daphne Clair	
ONE MAN, ONE LOVE	Natalie Fox	
LOVE'S LABYRINTH	Jessica Hart	
STRAW ON THE WIND	Elizabeth Power	
THE WINTER KING	Amanda Carpenter	
ADAM'S ANGEL	Lee Wilkinson	
RAINBOW ROUND THE MOON	Stephanie Wyatt	
DEAR ENEMY	Alison York	
LORD OF THE GLEN	Frances Lloyd	
OLD SCHOOL TIES	Leigh Michaels	

If you would like to order these books in addition to your regular subscription from Mills & Boon Reader Service please send £1.90 per title to: Mills & Boon Reader Service, Freepost, P.O. Box 236, Croydon, Surrey, CR9 9EL, quote your Subscriber No:................................. (If applicable) and complete the name and address details below. Alternatively, these books are available from many local Newsagents including W H Smith, J Menzies, Martins and other paperback stockists from 8 April 1994.

Name:...
Address:...
....Post Code:.........................

To Retailer: If you would like to stock M&B books please contact your regular book/magazine wholesaler for details.

You may be mailed with offers from other reputable companies as a result of this application.
If you would rather not take advantage of these opportunities please tick box ☐